"What aren't you telling me, Sophie? Are you keeping something secret about the night in the motel? You said we didn't have sex—"

"We didn't." She stopped and stared at him.

"Are you sure?" he pressed.

Sophie finally had to shake her head. "I honestly don't remember." That required a deep breath. "I have huge gaps in my memory from that night. And that's never happened to me before…"

"Me, either."

She hadn't meant to make a soft yeah-right mumble, but it just popped out. With Royce's hot cowboy looks, she was betting he'd had a one-night stand. Or a dozen.

"There's something else you're not telling me," Royce insisted.

Good grief. The man had ESP, or maybe his lawman's instincts were kicking in.

He tapped her right temple. "What is going on in your head? What are you keeping from me? Because I can promise you, it won't help. I need to hear everything that happened. Everything you remember…"

USA TODAY Bestselling Author

DELORES FOSSEN

STANDOFF AT MUSTANG RIDGE

HARLEQUIN®
entertain, enrich, inspire™

Recycling programs for this product may not exist in your area.

ISBN-13: 978-0-373-74716-0

STANDOFF AT MUSTANG RIDGE

Copyright © 2013 by Delores Fossen

This edition published by arrangement with Harlequin Books S.A.

For questions and comments about the quality of this book, please contact us at CustomerService@Harlequin.com.

® and TM are trademarks of Harlequin Enterprises Limited or its corporate affiliates. Trademarks indicated with ® are registered in the United States Patent and Trademark Office, the Canadian Trade Marks Office and in other countries.

www.Harlequin.com

Printed in U.S.A.

ABOUT THE AUTHOR

Imagine a family tree that includes Texas cowboys, Choctaw and Cherokee Indians, a Louisiana pirate and a Scottish rebel who battled side by side with William Wallace. With ancestors like that, it's easy to understand why USA TODAY bestselling author and former air force captain Delores Fossen feels as if she were genetically predisposed to writing romances. Along the way to fulfilling her DNA destiny, Delores married an air force top gun who just happens to be of Viking descent. With all those romantic bases covered, she doesn't have to look too far for inspiration.

Books by Delores Fossen

HARLEQUIN INTRIGUE

*Five-Alarm Babies
***Texas Paternity
***Texas Paternity: Boots and Booties
†Texas Maternity: Hostages
††Texas Maternity: Labor and Delivery
‡‡The Lawmen of Silver Creek Ranch

CAST OF CHARACTERS

Deputy Sheriff Royce McCall—He's the bad-boy lawman of Mustang Ridge, TX, who finds himself caught in the middle of a dangerous investigation with city girl Sophie Conway, a woman he knows he must resist. But his heart and body say otherwise.

Sophie Conway—Her attempts to do the right thing for her family put her in the path of a dangerous killer. She knows she can't do it alone, but Royce's involvement automatically makes him a target, too.

Travis Bullock—Sophie's ex-fiancé who's under investigation. He claims he still loves Sophie, but actions speak louder than words.

Sheriff Jake McCall—He wants to help his brother, Royce, but the investigation only gives him more questions than answers.

Stanton Conway—Sophie's half brother. Just how far would he go to save his family's ranch?

Eldon Conway—Even though he's Sophie's father, he's also a suspect in the attacks that have nearly left her dead.

Special Agent Keith Lott—He's deep in an investigation that could have dangerous consequences for Sophie and Royce.

Chapter One

Deputy Sheriff Royce McCall drew his Colt .45 and stepped behind the ice-crusted cottonwood tree.

Mercy.

He didn't need this. It was too cold for a gunfight or even an arrest, but he might have to deal with both.

He glanced out at the hunting cabin and especially at the sole window that was facing his direction. He didn't see any movement, but he'd seen footprints in the snow that someone had tried to cover up. Those footprints came from the woods and led straight to the cabin.

Hiding footprints usually wasn't a good sign.

Of course, anyone inside was trespassing since the cabin was on McCall land, but he'd sure take a trespasser over an armed robber.

Normally, Royce wouldn't have been concerned with suspected felons this far out since the cabin wasn't near any main roads and a good twenty miles from the town of Mustang Ridge. But a cop from Amarillo P.D. had called earlier to warn him of a bank-robbery suspect who might be in the area. The guy could have found his way here with plans to use it as a hideout.

Without taking his attention off the cabin, Royce eased his phone from his coat pocket. There wasn't enough signal strength to make a call in this remote location, but he fired off a text to his brother, Sheriff Jake McCall, to let him know about the possible situation.

A situation Royce would likely end up handling alone.

It would take at least a half hour for his brother to respond to the text and get Royce some backup all the way out here. With the temperature already below freezing and with the wind and snow spitting at him, he didn't want to wait another minute much less an hour—even if it meant he'd get a tongue-lashing from Jake.

Royce hoped that was all he got.

The Amarillo police had warned the fugitive was armed and dangerous.

Royce took that warning into account, pulled off the thick leather glove on his right hand so he'd have a better grip on the Colt, and he inched out from the cottonwood. Thankfully, there were other trees dotting the grounds, and he used them to make his way toward the cabin. He was nearly at the front when he heard something.

Movement inside.

So the person who'd tried to hide those footprints was definitely still around.

Royce used one of the porch posts for cover, but he knew there was a lot more of him exposed than there was hidden. He waited and listened, but the only sounds were the ragged wind and his own heartbeat crashing in his ears.

He'd been a deputy of Mustang Ridge for eleven years and had faced down an armed man or two, but it never got easier. If it ever did, Royce figured that'd be the time to quit and devote all his time to running his portion of the family ranch. Danger should never feel normal.

With his bare hand going numb, it was now or never. Steering clear of the window, he reached over and tested the knob.

It was locked.

Royce didn't issue any warnings. He turned and gave the door a swift kick, and even though it stayed on the hinges, the lock gave way, and it flew open. Before it even hit the wall, he had his gun ready and aimed.

He took in the place with a sweeping glance. Not much to take in, though. There was a set of bunk beds on one side, a small kitchen on the other and an equally small bathroom in the center back. Since the privacy curtain in the bathroom was wide-open, he could see straight inside. No one was there unless the person was in the shower.

Keeping a firm grip on his gun, Royce inched closer, and he heard some movement again.

Yeah, it was definitely coming from the shower stall.

He took a deep breath and made his way into the cabin so he could get a look inside the bathroom.

"I'll shoot," someone called out.

Royce froze. It was a woman—not the male robbery suspect he'd braced himself to face. However, it was hard to tell who the woman was with that quivery voice. Plus, he couldn't see much of her because the overhead lights weren't on, and the shower stall was hidden in the shadows.

Usually if threatened with violence, Royce would threaten right back. However, after one glance at her hand, the only part of her he could actually see, he realized a threat might not be the way to go.

Yeah, she was armed all right. She was holding a little Smith & Wesson, and it was possible she was even trying to aim the gun at him. But she was huddled in the tiny tiled shower, and her hand was shaking so hard she would have been lucky to hit him or anything else within ten feet of where she was trying to aim.

As his eyes adjusted to the darkness, he saw the woman was wearing an unbuttoned coat over what appeared to be a nightgown. No hat, no gloves, and those flat house shoes definitely weren't cold-weather gear. She had to be freezing.

"You need to put down that gun." Royce tried to keep his voice level and calm. Hard to do with the adrenaline pumping through him and the cold blasting at his back. She didn't look like much of a threat, but she was armed.

"I won't let you kill me," she said in a broken whisper.

"Kill you?" Jeez, what was going on here? "No one's going to kill you, lady. I'm hoping you've got the same idea when it comes to me and that Smith & Wesson you got wobbling around there."

She looked up at him as if confused by that remark, and when she took a single step out of the shower, her eyes met his.

Oh, man.

"Sophie?" And he cursed some more when he got a better look at her face. Yep, it was Sophie Conway, all right. A neighbor of sorts since her daddy, Eldon, owned the sprawling ranch next to his own family's land.

Sophie and Royce weren't exactly friends. All

right, they were pretty much on each other's bad side, but Royce still didn't think she'd shoot him.

He hoped he was right about that.

"It's me, Royce," he said in case by some miracle Sophie didn't recognize him. He leaned in a little so she could have a better look at him, and he maneuvered himself into a position so he could disarm her.

"I know who you are," Sophie said a split second before she tried to scramble away from him.

He blocked her path, which wasn't hard to do since the rest of her was as wobbly as her aim.

"Look, I'm not too happy about seeing you, either," Royce let her know, "but there's no reason for you to hold a grudge and point a gun at me."

Well, maybe there was a reason for the grudge part, but Royce wasn't getting into what'd happened between them four weeks ago.

"Are you drunk or something?" he asked.

She frowned, obviously not happy with that little conclusion. "What are you doing here?" She kept the gun pointed at him. "Did you come to kill me?"

Royce huffed. "No." He drew that out a few syllables. "I'm here because my family owns the cabin."

Sophie glanced around as if really seeing it for the first time. "This is your place?"

"Yeah." Again, Royce gave her a good dose

of his smart-mouth tone, something his brother, Jake, had told him he was pretty good at doing.

"I was out here looking for a couple of horses that broke fence, and maybe even an armed robber, so I decided to stop by and check on things. Now, care to tell me why you're here?"

Again, she looked around before her gaze came back to him, and while she was semi-distracted, Royce did something about that Smith & Wesson. He lunged at her and clamped his hands around her right wrist.

"No!" she shouted, and despite her shaky hands, she started fighting. "I need the gun."

Sophie kicked at him and tried to slug him with her left hand. She connected, sort of, her open hand slamming into his jaw.

And that's when Royce knew he'd had enough.

He knocked her hand against the sink, and her gun went flying into the sleeping part of the cabin at the same moment that she went flying at him. Even though he'd managed to disarm her, that didn't stop her from continuing the fight. She pushed and clawed at him, and he tossed his gun aside to stop it from being accidentally discharged in the fray.

Royce tried to subdue her without actually inflicting any bodily harm, but it was hard with Sophie fighting like a wildcat.

"Sophie, stop this now," he growled.

When she tried to knee him in the groin, Royce caught her, dragged her to the floor and flipped her onto her back. He pinned her body down with his.

Still, she didn't stop struggling.

She made one last attempt to toss him off her, and it was as if that attempt took all the fight from her. She went limp, and because he was so close to her face, just inches away, he saw the tears spring to her blue eyes.

Her eyes were still wide, and her chest was pumping for air, but at least she looked directly at him. "I won't let you kill me," she whispered. "I'm guessing you've got a bad hangover from a New Year's party, because you're not making any sense."

Man, they were back to the crazy talk. "I'm guessing you've got a bad hangover from a New Year's party, because you're not making any sense."

The new year was already two days past. Still, maybe she'd been on a bender. After all, she'd been pretty darn drunk the last time he'd seen her a month ago.

Blowing out a long breath, Royce caught onto her face so he could examine her eyes and the rest of her. Too bad *the rest of her* was what really caught his attention.

The struggle had done a number on her long dark brown hair, and strands of it were now on her damp cheek and neck. On him, too. Royce didn't want to feel anything other than anger and maybe some confusion when he looked at Sophie. But he failed at that, too.

He felt that kick of attraction.

The same stupid attraction that had gotten the better part of him four weeks ago when he'd had way too much to drink and run into her at a party. Royce had been nursing a bad attitude because his three-year-old niece had been so sick. Heaven knows what Sophie had been nursing, but she'd been as drunk as he was.

He should have remembered that huge amounts of liquor, a surly attitude and an attractive woman just didn't mix.

Especially this woman.

Sophie was too rich for his blood. Not that he was poor. Nope, his family had money, too, but they were basically ranchers. Sophie had been city-raised, and ever since she'd moved back to Mustang Ridge about a year ago, she had always seemed to turn up her nose at anything and anyone in the small ranching town that he called home.

Well, until that party at the Outlaw Bar.

She was the last person he'd expected to find stinkin' drunk, and that was the only explanation for why he'd ended up at the Lone Star Motel with her. Though his memories were a little blurry when it came to the details. The only thing that was clear was there'd been some clothing removed and a little intimate touching before they'd passed out.

"Wait a minute," Royce said, thinking back to that fiasco at the Outlaw Bar and the Lone Star Motel. "Do you think I came here to kill you because you told me to take a hike after you woke up that morning?" He didn't wait for an answer to that asinine question. "Because, Sophie, I got over that *fast*."

Besides, they hadn't been in a relationship or anything. They'd only been together that once, and when Sophie woke up that morning, she'd pitched a hissy fit.

"I told you to take a hike," she repeated. Sophie's forehead bunched up as if she was trying to recall that or something.

"You said you were about to get engaged, and if I came near you again, you'd file charges against me," he reminded her. His jaw tightened, and that cleared his head and body of any shred of lingering attraction. "Trust me, I got the message. I've got no time for a high-maintenance daddy's girl who won't own up to the fact that she got drunk and nearly had a dirty one-night stand with a cowboy cop."

She swallowed hard, stared at him.

Maybe he'd hurt her feelings. Well, he didn't give a rat's behind about that, but Royce did move away from her so he could stand up and get his body off hers, and then he could get her the heck out of his cabin and off his land.

He had enough memories of Sophie without making more.

"Why are you here?" he demanded. "And this time, don't give me a stupid answer about someone else or me trying to kill you." He tapped the badge clipped to his rawhide belt. "In case you've forgotten, I'm a deputy sheriff. I try to make a habit of not killing people—even ones who trespass on my land and point guns at me."

"I haven't forgotten who you are," Sophie murmured. She didn't say it with as much disdain as he'd expected, but there was a lot of unexpected stuff going on here today.

"Why. Are. You. Here?" he repeated.

Struggling and mumbling, she pushed herself to a sitting position. "Swear you aren't going to kill me."

"I swear," he snapped. He was about to chew her out for daring to ask him that, but Royce held back and just waited for her to continue.

"After I got the phone call...I started running." Sophie pulled in a hard breath, and by hanging on to the wall, she managed to get to her feet. "And this cabin was the first place I reached. I thought maybe I could hide until my father answered my text message." She paused, rubbed her forehead. "My phone doesn't work up here on the ridge."

That last part was the first thing she'd said that made a lick of sense. Cell service here was spotty at best. But it didn't explain why she'd run to the cabin in the first place. "What happened?"

Her gaze came to his, and her eyes widened. "Oh, God. We have to get out of here," she said, her voice trembling again. Heck, Sophie started trembling again, too. Shaking from head to toe.

Royce stepped in front of her when she tried to go toward the door.

"We can't stay," she insisted. "If they find us together, they'll try to kill him."

Great. Now they were back to her talking out of her head. Royce leaned in and took a whiff of her breath. No smell of booze, so maybe she had been drugged. Something was certainly off here.

"Okay, I'll bite," he snarled. "Who's the *him* that they'll try to kill?"

She pushed him aside and tried to get to her feet again. "The baby they believe I'm having," she mumbled.

Royce stared at her. "Wait a minute." He shook his head. "Are you pregnant?"

Sophie didn't answer right away. "No. But I told them I was."

Royce would get to the *them* part later, but for now he wanted more on the fake pregnancy claim. "Why the heck would you tell someone you're pregnant when you're not?"

Sophie groaned, a sound that came from deep within her throat. "I didn't have a choice. I thought it'd keep us alive."

Royce was sure that he blinked. "Us?"

The tears came to her eyes again. "*Us*," she verified. "I told them the baby was...yours."

He felt as if someone had slugged him—twice. "You what?" And that was the best he could manage. Royce just kept staring at her and probably would have continued if she hadn't latched on to him.

"I'm sorry, Royce. So sorry." Her breath caught in her throat. "But I just signed your death warrant."

Chapter Two

Sophie wished her teeth would stop chattering so she could hear herself think. Clearly, she'd been wrong about Royce wanting to kill her because he'd had more than ample opportunity to do that and hadn't. Of course, he might change his mind when he learned what she had done.

"My death warrant?" Royce snarled. He grabbed his dark brown Stetson that had fallen off during the scuffle and shoved it back on his head.

His jaw muscles were so tight that she didn't know how he managed to speak, but even without the words, Sophie could see his narrowed eyes. That, and every muscle in his body seemed primed for a fight. For answers, too.

Answers that Royce expected her to give him.

"We have to leave," she reminded him.

Even though her feet felt frozen to the floor, Sophie pushed her way past Royce and went to the front window so she could look out and keep watch. The bitter wind howling through the open door cut her bone-deep, but that was minor compared to everything else she was feeling.

"How did you get here?" she asked.

"My truck. It's parked over the ridge because the trail here isn't passable in winter." And that's all he said for several seconds. However, he did shut the door. "What did you mean about signing my death warrant?"

"Please, can we just go now and you can ask your questions once we're out of here?" But she stopped and realized if their positions were reversed, she would have dug in her heels. Just as Royce was doing now.

Maybe the partial truth wouldn't get them both killed. "I didn't want you involved in this, but I couldn't stop them—"

"Who are *them* and what is *this*?" he interrupted.

Sophie opened her mouth. Closed it. And she shook her head. Where was she to start? The beginning, maybe, but she wasn't even sure where the beginning was.

"About a month ago, my father arranged my marriage to his business partner, Travis Bullock—"

He cursed. "Sophie, how the heck is that related to my so-called death warrant?"

"It's related," she insisted. "I didn't love Travis, but my father said the marriage would ease some of his financial burdens. He had some investments that didn't pan out." She checked out the window again. "My late mother left me the entire estate. Long story," Sophie added in a mumble. "But I couldn't give or loan my father any money because the terms of my mother's will forbid it."

"I'd heard rumors of that." Royce paused a moment, waiting, and made an impatient circling motion with his fingers. He stooped, retrieved his Colt and slipped it back into the leather shoulder holster beneath his coat. He also put her gun in his pocket.

"Travis said that he'd cover my father's debts if I married him." Now it was Sophie's turn to pause. "He said he was in love with me and that he was willing to pay that price to have me."

Royce stared at her, and Sophie wished this meeting had been under different circumstances. She owed him a huge apology. Several of them, in fact.

"Royce," she muttered, her voice a whisper now. "I'm sorry."

"So you've said. It's not helping with this explanation. I still don't know what the heck is going on."

He gave her a scowl, the muscles stirring in a face that was far more handsome than she wanted it to be. Not that this would have been easier with a less attractive man, but those good looks—the coffee-brown hair and sizzling green eyes—had always unnerved her.

Attracted her, too.

Easy to attract in those cowboy-fit jeans, boots and Stetson. And it'd been that stupid attraction that had made her involve him in this equally stupid mess. Talk about a dangerous tangled web, and now she might have trapped Royce and her both in it.

Royce made another of those impatient sounds, and Sophie continued with what she hoped would be good enough answers to get them moving. "I started to have second thoughts about marrying Travis," she added. "He definitely wasn't the decent, honest man my father said he was."

"So, to get out of a loveless marriage," Royce concluded, his voice flat, "you told Travis we'd had sex and that you're pregnant with my baby?"

She nodded. It was more than that. Much more. But she instinctively knew that telling Royce all the details wasn't a good idea, especially since it didn't appear he was so furious with her that he was out to kill her.

"We didn't really have sex, did we?" he asked.

Sophie took a deep breath, shook her head.

Relief went through his eyes, and it wasn't a small amount of it, either. "Good. Because I was drunker than I'd ever been in my life, and I shouldn't have let things get that far."

"We didn't have sex," she snapped. "Now, just leave it at that, all right?"

"All right," he growled. "But Travis believes otherwise and he also believes we made a baby that night. Now he wants to kill us."

"Maybe," she mumbled. But again, that was just a small piece of the story. She turned back to the window and tried to assure herself that she hadn't been followed. "The reason I was trying to get out of the marriage was because I found out some things."

And here's where her explanation would have to veer off. She couldn't implicate her father in this.

Sophie chose her words carefully. "I believe Travis was into some illegal activity, and I was in the process of working with an FBI agent to uncover that activity. I was copying files and sending them to him."

Selective files, but that was yet something else Sophie wasn't about to tell a lawman who could, and would, arrest her father.

"Last night Travis confronted me and said he thought I was betraying him because I'd been acting suspicious." She glanced at Royce, ready to ask again if they could get moving, but he just motioned for her to continue. "I thought I'd settled his mind, but then after dinner, he confronted me again. He kept pushing for the truth, and the image of you flashed through my head."

Specifically, the image of them half-naked at the motel.

But she kept that to herself.

Best not to let Royce know that it was a particular image she couldn't get out of her mind. Or her dreams.

"And that's when you lied?" he asked.

She nodded, checked the window again. "More or less. I said I was pregnant with another man's child, and Travis told me he'd seen pictures of you and me together."

"Pictures?" Royce flatly repeated.

"I don't know if Travis had them or not, and he didn't show them to me. Maybe someone at the party at the Outlaw Bar took them." Or maybe they'd been a bluff.

"But these pictures convinced him that I'd gotten you pregnant." He paused. "Hell, I'm guessing Travis didn't take that news too well?"

"He didn't. He slapped me and stormed out."

Royce's jaw muscles jerked, tightening even more. "You should have had his sorry butt arrested for hitting you."

She'd wanted to. Heck, she'd wanted to slap Travis right back, but Sophie hadn't. Besides in

Travis's state of mind, he might have done a lot more than slap her.

"I thought it was over, that Travis was out of my life," Sophie continued. "Until this morning, that is. I got the call from the FBI agent." Just saying it required a deep breath. "He said he'd gotten word from a criminal informant that someone had hired a hit man to go after you and that someone else had been hired to kidnap me."

Royce stood there, staring, with his forehead bunched up. It was a lot to take in. She'd had several hours and still hadn't managed it.

"I told the agent I was going to call you," she continued when Royce didn't say anything. "I wanted to warn you, but the agent said I shouldn't."

"Because he thought you might be trying to kill me, too."

"Really?" No more bunched-up forehead. Instead, Royce rolled his eyes and cursed. "And why is that? Why wouldn't I need to know something like that?"

Royce's cursing got worse. "Why the hell would you believe I'd want to kill you?"

"Because the agent said Travis might have convinced you to do it."

In hindsight, it wasn't a good reason, but it had made some sense at the time. In her terrified mind, Sophie had figured that Travis was angry enough to convince Royce that she'd trapped him into this pregnancy. Her fears hadn't calmed a bit when Royce had shown up at the cabin with his gun aimed at her.

"Why didn't the FBI send someone to the ranch to protect you?" Royce asked. "And why the hell didn't they call me or my brother to tell us what was going on?"

"I don't know. I wasn't thinking straight, and maybe the FBI had someone on the way. I'm not sure. Right after the phone call, I looked out the window and saw two men dressed all in black. They both had rifles."

After several more moments of his intense stare, some of the skepticism left Royce's eyes. "You should have called me then and there."

"Maybe. But remember, I was still of the mind-set that you might want to do me in for ruining your life and getting you in hot water with Travis."

"I can handle Travis," he snarled. "And later I'll want to know why this FBI agent put such crazy ideas in your head."

Sophie wanted to know the same thing. Of course, she could have misinterpreted what the agent had said since she'd never been that scared in her life.

"Why didn't you just hide or yell for your father when you saw those two armed gunmen?"

Royce asked. "Certainly, he's got a ton of men around the ranch?"

"Normally. But most are still on holiday break. Plus, he let some hands go because, well, to save money. I don't know where my father and brother are, but I realized I was in the house alone. I got dressed, grabbed the Smith & Wesson and left."

He glanced at her gown, silently challenging that getting dressed part.

"I *partially* dressed," Sophie amended with a huff. "And I hurried out from the other side of the house so the men wouldn't see me. I started running and ended up here." She'd more or less stumbled her way to the cabin.

Royce opened his mouth to say something, but then he cursed again when his phone buzzed. He jerked it from his coat pocket as if he'd declared war on it and looked at the screen.

"Trouble?" she asked, holding her breath.

"My brother. He's just checking on me." He replied to the text, and he shoved the phone back in his pocket. "I told him I was on my way back to town and that he was to send a deputy to your father's ranch." Royce looked at her. "You need to come with me to the sheriff's office so I can take your statement."

A statement with more questions than answers. Had Travis really sent two gunmen to kidnap her because she'd told him she was pregnant with Royce's child?

Or was this about something else?

"I'll have Travis brought in for questioning, too," Royce added. He went to the porch, motioning for her to stay back, and he looked around the area. Not an ordinary look. The thorough kind a cop would do.

Finally, he motioned for her to follow him. "I'll need to speak to this FBI agent, too. What's his name?"

"Keith Lott."

Royce repeated it as if trying to figure out if he'd heard it before. "How'd you meet him?"

"He contacted me. Lott asked me to help him look into Travis's business files, and since I was suspicious, I agreed to help him."

Plus, she wanted a way out of the marriage.

"I'll also need to talk to your father," Royce insisted.

Sophie went stiff. "He didn't have anything to do with this."

"There had to be a reason he wasn't at the ranch this morning."

"But that reason has nothing to do with those two gunmen," she countered.

Royce made a skeptical sound. "I'll still be questioning him. Can you walk down the ridge?" he asked before she could respond to that.

"I'd crawl if it means getting out of here."

"Crawling's not necessary, but I don't want you falling. Those shoes aren't exactly meant for trekking through snow and ice."

She nodded, knowing he was right, but she'd grabbed the first pair she could find. Sophie caught onto the back of Royce's jacket as he led them out of the cabin. They both continued to keep watch.

"Why aren't you chewing me out because of the lie I told?" she whispered.

He lifted his shoulder. "Desperate people do desperate things."

Yes, she had indeed been desperate. "I honestly didn't think it would make Travis come after you. And me."

Royce didn't respond to that. He kept trudging through the ice and snow that blanketed the trail, but she figured he was chewing her out in his mind.

She certainly was.

Mercy, she'd been so stupid to blurt that out and even more stupid to have agreed to the marriage in the first place. Of course, her father hadn't given her much of a choice about the marriage.

Soon, she'd have to figure out how to handle her father's situation, too.

Royce stopped so quickly that Sophie plowed

right into him, and he turned, caught onto her to stop her from falling. She was about to ask him why he'd stopped, but he put his finger to his mouth in a "stay quiet" gesture.

And he reached into his jacket and drew his gun.

That robbed her of her breath, and her gaze darted around so she could see what had alarmed him. But Sophie didn't see anything other than the winter landscape. Didn't hear anything, either, but that wasn't surprising since the wind was starting to howl now.

Royce lifted his head just a fraction, and without warning, he latched on to her arm and threw her to the ground. The impact nearly knocked the breath right out of her.

Sophie didn't have time to ask why he'd done that, because she heard something. Someone was moving in the trees behind them. And that sound barely had time to register when the shot blasted through the air.

Chapter Three

A dozen things went through Royce's mind, but first and foremost was to get Sophie out of the line of fire. He dragged her behind the nearest tree. When he looked out, ready to return fire, he saw nothing.

But someone was definitely out there.

The shot was proof of that.

Royce figured it was too much to hope that it was a hunter who'd fired a stray shot. No, he wasn't that lucky. However, he wasn't sure he believed all of Sophie's story about hit men and kidnappers.

That left her ex, Travis.

Royce hardly knew the man since Travis had only moved to Mustang Ridge about a year ago, but maybe Travis was the sort who'd let his temper take him to a bad place when Sophie had told him about the fake pregnancy. If so, Travis was going to pay, and pay hard for this.

A bullet slammed into the tree just inches from

where Royce and Sophie were, and he pushed her even lower to the ground until her face was right against the snow.

"I'm Deputy Sheriff McCall," Royce shouted out just on the outside chance those two bullets hadn't been meant for him.

Another shot smacked into the tree.

Well, that cleared up his *outside chance* theory that the shooter wasn't trying to kill him or Sophie. Or both.

"Travis?" Royce tried again. "If that's you, we can settle this without me having to shoot you."

And there was no mistaking, Royce would take out whoever was doing this if he didn't stop. Royce waited for an answer. No shot this time, but he did hear something else. Footsteps.

And he cursed.

Because from the sound of it, there wasn't just one set but two. Hell. Had Sophie been right about those kidnapper–hit men being after her? If so, maybe the shots were meant to pin them in place so the men could sneak up on them, kill Royce and kidnap her.

That wasn't going to happen, either.

"Stay down," Royce growled when Sophie tried to lift her head.

Sophie was shaking, and her teeth were still chattering, but Royce couldn't take the time to reassure her. Not that he could have done that anyway since there was nothing reassuring about this mess. He had to focus every bit of his attention on those footsteps. Not easy to do with the wind rattling the bare tree branches and his own pulse making a crashing noise in his ears.

A fourth shot zinged past Sophie and him.

The angle was different, and using that angle, Royce tried to pinpoint the location of the shooter—directly ahead but moving slightly to the right. He hoped like the devil that it didn't mean the second one was going to the left, but it's what his brother and he would do if they were trying to close in on someone they wanted to capture.

Royce made a quick peek around the cottonwood and saw a blur of motion as the gunman ducked behind another tree. *Mercy,* the guy was getting close, and that probably meant the one on his blind side was, too.

He reached behind him with his left hand and pulled out the Smith & Wesson that he'd gotten away from Sophie earlier. Without taking his attention off the woods, he dragged her to a sitting position and put the gun in her hand.

"Watch that direction," he said, tipping his head to the right. He positioned her so that his body was still shielding her as much as possible. "If you see one of the men, don't hesitate. Shoot."

It wasn't a stellar plan, especially since Royce

had no idea if Sophie had any experience with firearms. Plus, she was still shaking, and that wouldn't help her aim.

But he didn't have a choice.

They could both die if one of the gunmen managed to ambush them. Too bad he hadn't told his brother to send out backup, but until that first shot had been fired, Royce hadn't known that things were going from bad to worse.

He didn't have a lot of extra ammunition so he couldn't just start firing warning shots, but Royce waited, trying to time it just right for the best impact. He listened to the sound of that movement on his left. Honed in on it. Aimed.

And fired.

Royce's shot blistered through the winter air, and it slammed into something. Not into a man from the sound of it, but the footsteps and shuffling around stopped. Royce could have sworn everything stopped because things suddenly became eerily still.

The seconds crawled by, and because Sophie's arm was right against his, he could feel her tense muscles. Her breathing became shallow, too. Royce risked glancing at her just to make sure she was all right. She looked exactly as he'd expected her to look.

Terrified.

But her eyes seemed more focused, and she had a solid grip on the gun.

"McCall?" someone shouted.

Royce didn't answer. He just waited to see what would happen next, but it was a little unnerving to hear this killer wannabe use his name.

"We don't want you," the shooter added a moment later. "We want the woman. Let her go, and we won't hurt you."

Right.

They wouldn't kill a lawman, the only witness to their crime of kidnapping? Plus, there was that whole disturbing part about what these bozos planned to do with Sophie. Royce doubted they had friendly intentions.

But Sophie moved to get up anyway.

Royce cursed and shoved her right back down.

He gave her a "what the heck are you doing?" look.

"They want me, not you," she mouthed.

He gave her another look, a scowl, to let her know she was wrong about that. "They shot at *us*," Royce reminded her in a whisper.

And the gunmen no doubt wanted to fire more of those shots at point-blank range. Royce had no intentions of dying in these woods today and allowing Sophie to be taken God knows where so that Travis could do God knows what to her. Royce risked another peek around the tree, but the gunman he'd seen earlier was nowhere in sight.

"McCall!" the man shouted again. "Hand her over to us. This ain't your fight."

Yeah, it was, and it had become his fight the exact second that first shot had been fired. Or maybe even earlier when he'd walked in on Sophie in the cabin. Either way, Royce wasn't backing down.

The footsteps started again. The guys must have given up on their attempt to lure him into surrendering.

"Get ready," Royce whispered to Sophie.

She did. With every part of her still shaking, she scooted back up and aimed the gun to her right. Royce adjusted his aim, too, and he calculated each of those footsteps. Without warning, he leaned out and fired.

This time, the shot hit human flesh.

Royce was familiar enough with that deadly sounding thud. The man groaned in pain. Then cursed a blue streak. So, he'd been wounded, not killed, and that meant he was still dangerous. Plus, his uninjured partner was out there somewhere, no doubt closing in on them.

"Trade places with me," Royce quietly instructed Sophie.

And despite her shakiness, she managed to work her way beneath him and to the side of the tree where the injured gunman was. Royce was counting on whatever wound he'd given the guy, that it'd be serious enough to affect the guy's shooting ability.

Royce braced himself for whatever was about to happen, and he added a prayer that he could get both Sophie and him out of this alive.

Then he heard another sound.

Not footsteps. It was coming from behind them, and it was the sound of a vehicle driving up on the ranch trail.

Great.

This could be very bad if the gunmen had some kind of backup, which would make sense since they'd need a way of getting Sophie off this ridge. But their backup would also likely be armed and just as dangerous.

Royce turned, adjusting his position so he could try to cover both his right and behind them. He figured there was a high potential to hit one and miss the other, but he didn't have options here. He just had to wait and put his bullets to the best use.

"I'm sorry," Sophie whispered.

Since that sounded like some kind of goodbye, Royce didn't even acknowledge it. "Keep watch," he ordered.

Behind them, he heard the vehicle crunch to a stop on the icy trail, and the driver turned off the engine. The movement from the gunmen was mixed with the sound of the vehicle door opening and closing. That pretty much put Royce's heart right in his throat, but even that wasn't going to make him accept Sophie's goodbye.

"Royce?" he heard someone call out. "Where are you?"

The relief was instant because it was his brother, Jake. Sophie and he had backup, but he didn't want Jake walking into gunfire.

"Here," Royce shouted back. "There are two shooters," he warned his brother.

Just as Royce had expected, that brought on more gunfire. Not one single shot at a time, but blasts from both their right and left. Sophie and he dropped down onto their sides, and back to back they both took aim.

And fired.

Royce didn't stop with one shot, either. He sent three bullets in the direction of his gunman, and following his lead, Sophie did the same.

"I'm coming up behind you," Jake called out to them. "And more backup's on the way."

The gunmen probably didn't like the sound of that, and even though they continued firing, Royce caught a glimpse of the guy at his side. He'd turned and was moving back. No doubt trying to get out of there fast since his partner and he were now outgunned.

Royce sent another bullet his way, hoping it would cause him to dive to the ground. He didn't want the goon firing any more bullets in Sophie's direction, but he also wanted the men captured and arrested. That way, Jake and he could get answers about why this fiasco had started in the first place.

"I'm Sheriff Jake McCall," his brother shouted. "Put down your weapons now!"

The warning was standard procedure, but like before, the gunmen just kept firing.

Behind Sophie and Royce a shot rang out.

Jake, no doubt.

And the bullets began to pelt the trees and ground ahead of them. Still, Royce didn't hear the sound he wanted to hear—the gunmen surrendering or at least falling to the ground, wounded and incapable of shooting back.

Sophie kept hold of her gun, but she also put her left hand over her head, maybe because the blasts were deafening. However, it could be because she was about to fall apart. Royce was betting this was the first time in her privileged life that she'd been on the receiving end of gunfire, and he was surprised that she'd been able to handle this much.

Suddenly the shots stopped.

The silence crawled through the woods, and it took Royce a moment to focus on what was happening around him. Jake was there. Behind them and to his right. He'd stopped firing, as well.

Then Jake cursed.

Royce did, too.

"What's wrong?" Sophie asked. There was little sound in her voice, and her eyes were wide with renewed fear when she came up with the answer to her own question.

The gunmen were getting away.

"Get Sophie out of here," Royce told his brother. "I'm going after them."

Chapter Four

Sophie couldn't sit down. She was too worried to do anything except pace, but she was also exhausted and didn't know how much longer her legs would last. The spent adrenaline and raw nerves were really doing a number on her, and if she sat down, she might collapse.

Or explode.

She'd been pacing in the Mustang Ridge Sheriff's Office for well over an hour now, since Deputy Maggie McCall had arrived at the cabin to drive her back to town. And during that time Royce and his brother, Jake, had been out looking for the men who'd tried to kill them.

Sophie was beyond worried. Those men were kidnappers at best, killers at worst, and now Royce and Jake were in danger because of her.

"The McCall men know how to take care of themselves," Maggie said when she handed Sophie a cup of coffee.

Sophie mumbled her thanks for both the coffee

and the reassurance, took the cup and watched the deputy return to the window. Maggie checked her phone, too, as if making sure she hadn't missed a call from her husband. Sophie didn't know Maggie McCall, but the tall blonde seemed just as rattled as Sophie was.

Since it was better than pacing or fidgeting, Sophie checked her own phone for any missed calls and messages. Nothing. She tried again to reach Travis, but again it went straight to voice mail. So did the call she made to Agent Keith Lott. She tried not to read anything into the agent's response.

Or lack of it.

After all, there were plenty of dead spots for reception around Mustang Ridge, and it was possible Lott was somewhere in the area, helping the McCalls with the investigation. But it did bother Sophie that Agent Lott hadn't personally called her or shown up at the sheriff's office. He certainly knew about the danger because he'd been the one to warn her that the two men were on the way to her house to kidnap her.

So where was Lott now?

She prayed that a gunman or two hadn't been sent after him, as well. It was possible. Anything was. Because Sophie had no idea what was going on.

"I didn't mean for any of this to happen," Sophie mumbled.

"So you've said." Maggie kept her attention nailed to the window and Main Street. "And you didn't get a good look at either gunman."

It wasn't exactly a question, but judging from her tone, the deputy wasn't pleased that Sophie had kept quiet about the circumstances leading up to the attack. Truth was, there wasn't much more she could tell Maggie other than she had gotten a warning from Agent Lott that she was in danger, and in that frantic, crazy state of mind, she'd run to the cabin where Royce had found her.

Sophie had left out the details of the info she'd been providing to Lott. She also left out the fact that she'd lied about being pregnant with Royce's baby. And the drunken encounter she'd had with Royce the previous month. She'd included barebones information in the written statement that Maggie had insisted on taking. But Sophie wasn't sure how long she could keep her secrets.

Or even if keeping secrets was the right thing to do.

Because it might have been her lie that had put Royce in danger in the first place.

"Finally," Maggie said. She practically dropped her coffee cup on her desk, and she raced to throw open the door when the truck came to a stop in front of the office.

Sheriff Jake McCall came in first. Unharmed, thank God. Sophie held her breath waiting for Royce, and when he stepped inside, she knew from his face that the pursuit of the gunmen had not gone well.

"I was worried." Maggie pulled her husband to her and kissed him. Jake took the time to kiss her back before he let go and turned to Sophie.

"The gunmen got away," he informed her.

Sophie had figured as much since they'd returned alone and because Royce was scowling. It was bad news because now they couldn't question the men and find out who'd sent them.

Of course, her money was on Travis.

Royce skimmed his gaze over her, his attention pausing on the jeans and sweater she was wearing.

"Maggie loaned them to me," she explained. And even though it was minor in the grand scheme of things, Sophie was glad she hadn't had to wait around the sheriff's office in her nightgown.

"The Rangers are still out searching for the men, and they have a CSI team in the woods to collect blood samples from the one that Royce wounded," Jake explained. He, too, looked at Sophie. "And on the drive back from town, Royce called your father and brother. They said they were in Amarillo on business and will get here as fast as they can."

"Business," she repeated. Neither had mentioned a trip to Amarillo, but then there wasn't a lot of information being shared at their house these days. She certainly hadn't told them she'd been providing information to an FBI agent.

"Royce called Agent Lott, too," Jake continued. "They're all coming in so we can try to get this straight."

"You actually spoke to Agent Lott?" Sophie hadn't expected to hear that. "Is he all right?"

"Why wouldn't he be?" Jake asked.

"He didn't answer my calls. In fact, I haven't heard a word from him since he warned me of the gunmen who were going to try to kidnap me."

Royce's scowl deepened. "Lott's on the way. But Travis didn't answer his phone so I left a message for him."

It probably wasn't a pleasant message. *Good.* She certainly didn't plan on saying anything nice to him. If he came in, that is. Maybe Travis had realized that the authorities were onto him and had fled.

Royce turned to his brother and Maggie who still had her arm around her husband's waist. "Why don't you head back home?" Royce suggested. "I'll question Sophie's father and brother. And I'll talk to the FBI agent."

Jake shook his head, but before he could say anything, Royce added, "You're on your honeymoon for Pete's sake. It's bad enough you didn't take a trip, but neither of you should be working." He glanced at Sophie. "They got married just three days ago."

Sophie had heard something about that. She'd also heard the sheriff's young daughter was recovering from leukemia or something similar and that's why there'd been no honeymoon.

"We do need to get ready for Sunny's trip to the hospital," Maggie said to her husband.

"Hospital?" Sophie asked. "I thought her condition was improving."

Jake nodded. "It is. She just needs another treatment, and it'll require a couple of days' stay in the hospital. She'll be admitted first thing in the morning."

"And that's all the more reason for you to leave now," Royce insisted. "I doubt the gunmen will show up here, and if I need help, I can call in Billy."

Billy Kilpatrick, the deputy. While she was pacing, Sophie had seen his nameplate on one of the desks. Sophie hoped the deputy was nearby and capable of providing backup, because she agreed about Jake and Maggie leaving. They obviously had enough to deal with already.

Maggie and Jake exchanged glances before he finally nodded. "Call me if anything comes up," he told Royce.

Royce assured his brother that he would, and Jake and his bride wasted no time getting out of there. Sophie couldn't help but notice they were practically wrapped around each other as they hurried to Maggie's car. A couple in love and hotly attracted to each other.

She envied them.

And then Sophie looked at Royce. Remembered the attraction that she shouldn't be feeling. Or even thinking about. Fortunately, the surly look he was giving her was a different reminder—that he wasn't pleased about any part of their situation other than maybe being alive.

"I'm sorry," Sophie said right off, and she figured she could say it a thousand more times, and it still wouldn't be enough. "I need to make this right."

That deepened his scowl even more. "That's what I'm trying to do."

"But I can do something, too. I called Travis and left a message, telling him we have to talk. I have to let him know I lied about the pregnancy."

"What makes you think he'll believe you?" Royce locked the door, took a magazine clip from his drawer and reloaded. "Travis will probably just think you're lying now, so you won't be kidnapped."

Oh, mercy. Royce might be right. Still, she had to try. "I'll agree to take a pregnancy test."

"Results can be faked?" Royce huffed, scrubbed his hand over his face. "Look, if Travis sent these men after us—and I believe he did—then, he's not going to listen to reason. He's riled to the core and wants to get back at you. At us," he amended.

She couldn't argue with that. "But eventually he'll know I've lied."

"Yeah, and by then it might be too late. Just because the two gunmen failed at kidnapping you, it doesn't mean he won't send someone else."

That was a stark reminder that Sophie didn't need. "I have to do something to stop you from being in danger."

"Too late. We're both targets, and despite what the gunman said about wanting only you, I don't believe that for a minute. Any of those shots they fired could have killed either or both of us."

Sophie knew that, of course, but it somehow made it worse to hear the words spoken aloud. "I'm so sorry." Her voice cracked, and she felt the tears burn her eyes.

She hated the tears. And herself. She had made such a mess of things.

"I don't want you talking to Travis," Royce insisted. "Especially not alone. And I don't want another apology," he snapped when she opened her mouth.

Sophie had indeed been about to repeat how sorry she was, but words weren't going to make this all go away.

Royce cursed when his attention landed on the tears she was trying to blink back, and he caught onto her arm and had her sit in the chair next to his desk. He dropped down across from her.

"I don't want tears, either," he grumbled. Then he huffed. "Crying won't help." His voice was softer now, but it was loaded with frustration.

Sophie bit her lip, trying to force herself not to cry. It didn't make it easier that Royce was right in her face, mere inches away. Not only could she see those intense green eyes, she could see every detail of his features.

And she took in his scent, too.

He smelled like the winter woods mixed with his own musky warmth.

That scent, his *warmth*, stirred something in her mind. Just a glimpse of a memory. Of Royce and her falling into bed. For that split second, she could feel the mattress against her back. And more. She could feel Royce's weight on her. The sensation of that hit her hard, and she choked back a sound that was part gasp, part moan.

She shouldn't be reacting or voicing that reaction to something that was probably just a mixed-up dream. After all, when she'd awakened that morning, Royce hadn't been on top of her.

"Sophie?" she heard Royce say. "Where are you right now? Because, believe me, this conversation is far more important than anything you're thinking about."

True. But it still took her a moment to push the sensations aside. That, and the blasted tears that kept coming to her eyes.

"I'm not usually a crier," she mumbled. There was no way she'd address his comment about what was on her mind. Because *Royce* was what was on her mind.

"Well, you're probably not used to coming so close to dying." He paused. "Most people would cry in your situation. It's just that tears bother me. My mom was a crier," he added so quickly that his words ran together.

Sophie remembered her father saying something about Royce's parents having a bad marriage before Mrs. McCall passed away from breast cancer.

"Tears remind you of your mother's illness?" she speculated.

"No. They just remind me of how unhappy she was. And we're getting off the subject here." He caught onto her shoulders. "What aren't you telling me, Sophie? Are you keeping something secret about the night in the motel? You said we didn't have sex—"

"We didn't." She stopped and stared at him.

"Did we?" he pressed.

Sophie finally had to shake her head. "I honestly don't remember." That required a deep breath. "I have huge gaps in my memory from that night. And that's never happened to me before. I don't get drunk and sleep with people I hardly know."

"Me, either."

She hadn't meant to make a soft yeah-right mumble, but it just popped out. With Royce's hot cowboy looks, she was betting he'd had a one-night stand. Or a dozen.

"I don't sleep with women who aren't my type," he clarified. But then he cursed, waved that off. "It's not an insult. I'm sure I'm not your type, either."

He wasn't. Well, not her usual type anyway, but Sophie could still feel herself go warm when she thought of his kisses. Now *those* she remembered. And his body. That's because he'd been stark naked when she'd woken up in bed with him.

"There's something else you're not telling me," Royce insisted.

Good grief. The man had ESP, or maybe his lawman's instincts were kicking in.

He tapped her right temple. "What is going on in your head? What are you keeping from me? Because I can promise you, it won't help. I need to hear everything that happened. Everything you remember because it could help us figure out how to bring Travis down."

She desperately wanted to stop Travis. But freedom from Travis came with a huge price tag.

"Can I tell you something off the record?" she asked.

Royce looked at her as if her ears were on backward. "Excuse me?"

"Off the record," she repeated. "As in you don't put it in a report, and you don't mention a word of it to anyone, even your brother."

Dead silent, Royce continued to stare at her. "What the hell is going on?"

Sophie didn't back down. Yes, she was still trembling from the attack, but this was critical.

"You won't tell anyone," she insisted.

He stared. She waited. And the seconds crawled by before Royce finally nodded.

Sophie searched his eyes for any sign he was lying. She didn't see anything but the renewed anger and frustration. Too bad. She'd rather that than an arrest warrant.

"When I was going through Travis's files," she

said, and she had to take another deep breath and give herself some time to choose her words, "I found some papers that could possibly paint my father in a bad light."

Yes, that was sugarcoating it, but she had to be careful with what she said.

He blinked, paused and then cursed. "Bad light? You mean he did something illegal." And it wasn't a question.

Suddenly the tears were gone and she knew what she had to do. Sophie moved closer because she wanted him to see the determination in her own eyes. Determination not to say or confirm anything that would put her father behind bars.

"I love my father," she settled for saying. "And the only reason I just told you about the papers was so you'd have a complete picture."

Royce shook his head and took her by her shoulders again. "There's nothing complete about that. What do these papers have to do with the fact that someone tried to kill us?"

Nothing.

She hoped.

But Sophie didn't get a chance to say that. She heard the doorknob rattle, and her gaze flew in that direction.

And her heart went to her knees.

Travis was standing there, looking right at them through the reinforced glass. Except he was giving them more a glare, and he hadn't missed the close contact between Royce and her. In fact, Royce's hands had been on her.

Royce shoved her behind him. In the same motion, he drew his gun.

"Call off your cowboy, Sophie," Travis said, his voice a dangerous warning. His eyes were narrowed to slits. "Or things are going to get ugly fast."

Chapter Five

Royce hadn't expected to agree with Travis, but the man was right about one thing—things were about to get ugly.

Travis was clearly upset. Royce was already past that stage, and he glared back at the man who was glaring at him.

"I'll go with him," Sophie insisted. "I don't want a fight."

Well, Royce did. He wanted to beat this moron to a pulp if he was the one who'd hired those gunmen. And Royce was leaning in the direction of that *if* being highly likely.

"You're not going with him," Royce insisted, and he shot her a warning glance over his shoulder. "Stay put. I'll handle this. And then we'll finish that conversation about your father."

Sophie swallowed hard, but he wasn't sure she would actually listen to him. She was turning out to be a lot more stubborn than he'd thought she would be, and his expectations in that area had been pretty darn high.

With his gun drawn and ready, Royce went to the door, unlocked it and threw it open. He gave Travis a quick once-over and didn't see any visible weapons. However, the man was wearing a thick winter coat, and he could hide lots of things under that.

"I heard about the shooting, and I got here as fast as I could," Travis volunteered. "How's Sophie?"

Royce ignored him and his question. "You don't mind if I frisk you for weapons, huh?" Royce asked, and he didn't wait for an answer or permission.

He took Travis by the arm, pulled him inside and practically shoved him against the desk. Royce also kicked the door shut and relocked it. He doubted Travis would turn and run, but he didn't want to risk those gunmen storming the place while he was distracted with Travis.

"This isn't necessary," Travis complained.

"Humor me," Royce fired back. It didn't take him long to locate the gun in the slide holster at Travis's back, and Royce disarmed him.

Travis whirled back around to face him. "I have a permit to carry that concealed."

Royce would check on that to make sure it was true. "Your permit doesn't extend to bringing weapons, concealed or otherwise, in the sheriff's office. Especially since you're a suspect in an attempted-murder investigation."

"What?" Travis's hands went on his hips, and his attention shot to Sophie. "You think I had something to do with this attack?"

"Did you?" Sophie asked.

Travis was breathing through his mouth now, and his face was flushed. In fact, everything about him looked ill-tempered and out of sorts. The wind had chapped his face and mouth and torn through his normally styled reddish-brown hair. He still had on his usual fancy rich clothes—a suit, matching overcoat and shoes that probably cost more than Royce's entire wardrobe—but everything looked askew.

Maybe because his murder-for-hire plot hadn't worked.

"No, of course I didn't have anything to do with the attack," Travis told her. "You're my fiancée, Sophie. I don't have a reason to hurt you."

"Really?" And Royce didn't bother to keep the sarcasm out of that one-word question. "She's your *ex-fiancée,* and you assaulted her when she told you she was carrying another man's child."

A muscle jumped in Travis's jaw, and his narrowed dust-colored eyes shifted from Sophie to Royce. "I was upset. Stunned. You would have reacted the same way if you'd been in my position."

"No. Hell, no, I wouldn't. I don't hit women even when I'm stunned and upset." Royce stepped closer. Since he was a good six inches taller than Travis, Royce hoped he looked as riled and intimating as he felt. "I especially wouldn't hire two dirt wads to kidnap or kill her."

"I didn't do that!" Travis insisted. He tried to move toward Sophie, but Royce blocked his path. Travis huffed. "I'm here to apologize, Sophie. I love you, and I still want us to get married."

A burst of air left Sophie's mouth. "You slapped me."

"Only because of those pictures." He shifted uneasily. "And because of the pregnancy. Honestly, how did you expect me to react? I know you slept with him before we got engaged, but it still stung."

Royce didn't miss the *way* Travis said *him*. As if Royce were something lower than pond scum. Well, Royce didn't think too highly of him, either.

Of course, there was something a whole lot bigger in Travis's weasely justification for his reaction. There was that lying part about Royce and Sophie sleeping together.

Or *maybe* it was a lie.

Sophie had admitted to having blank spots in

her memory. Royce had them, too, but he figured even if he was drunk off his butt, he'd remember sleeping with a woman like Sophie.

"Did you hear me, Sophie?" Travis said. "I was jealous that you'd slept with him, and I lost control for just that split second."

Sophie opened her mouth, no doubt to spill the baby lie, but Royce gave a "keep quiet" glare. Travis would learn the truth soon enough, but Royce wanted a few answers first. And he hoped his request for silence in that area didn't have anything to do with tormenting Travis.

Though it probably did.

Even if by some miracle Travis was innocent of hiring those gunmen, Royce still wanted the moron to squirm for slapping Sophie.

"You told Sophie you had pictures of me and her," Royce tossed out there.

Travis nodded. "Someone sent them to me. I don't know who," he said before Royce could ask. "There was no return address on the envelope, and it was postmarked from Amarillo."

"I want to see them." Because seeing them might tell Royce who took them. That was the start to finding out why, and it might shed some light on the attack. It might also prove that Travis was lying about the photos and the hit men.

"They're at my office," Travis explained. Royce blocked him again when he tried to step around him and get closer to Sophie. "Call some-one. Have them brought over."

Travis clearly didn't like that particular order, or maybe his increased scowl was for the body block Royce was putting on him. "There's no one in my office right now. I'll bring them back later today."

"You could do that, *if* I don't arrest you," Royce reminded him. "Right now, I'm thinking your arrest is a given."

The man's shoulders snapped back. "You don't have any proof to make an arrest. Because there's not any evidence against me. Sophie?" Travis mumbled some profanity. "Can you tell this cow-boy I wouldn't hurt you? I just want to work things out with you."

"Work out things?" Royce questioned. "What about the pictures and the baby?"

"I forgive her." But Travis's teeth were clenched when he said it, and that wasn't a forgiving look in his eyes.

Before Royce could stop her, Sophie walked closer. She stopped at Royce's side and kept her attention nailed to her scowling ex. "I'm not sure I can trust you, Travis."

"You can't," Royce insisted.

But Sophie and Travis kept their eyes locked.

"I can regain your trust," he assured her.

Royce was about to disagree, but something

caught his attention. A dark blue car came to a stop directly behind his truck that was parked in front of the office. He didn't recognize the vehicle, but he knew the two men who stepped from it.

Sophie's half brother and her father, Stanton and Eldon Conway.

"After all," Travis said, his gaze drifting toward the visitors who were making their way to the door. "Look at what I'm doing to help you and your father."

Even though Royce wasn't touching Sophie, he could almost feel her muscles tense. He definitely heard the change in her breathing. Travis's tone had been nonthreatening, but there was indeed a threat just below the surface.

"Yes," Sophie mumbled. She looked up at Royce, and he knew she was about to do something stupid. Or rather she'd try.

"You're not going with him," Royce let her know. "Yeah, I know he agreed to pay off your father's debts, but that's not worth your life."

"Deputy," Travis said. His tone was now placating. "I love Sophie, and her life isn't in danger as long as she's with me."

Royce went with a little placating attitude himself. "Someone hired two men to kidnap her. And those two men then fired a boatload of shots at her. Now, if you didn't hire those men, then who the hell did?"

Travis's mouth quivered, threatening to smile, and he hitched his thumb to the door just as Stanton tested the knob and then knocked.

"Why don't you ask them that question?" Travis insisted. "Because if you want to pin the blame for this on someone, both of them have a much bigger motive for kidnapping Sophie than I do."

Oh, he didn't like that smug look or the sound of this. "What motive?" Royce demanded.

"Ask Eldon." And this time, Travis didn't fight the smile. He grinned like a confident man. "I'm sure if you press Sophie's father as hard as you're pressing me, he'll tell you all about it."

SWEET HEAVEN. THIS WAS exactly what Sophie had been trying to avoid, and yet here was her father at the sheriff's office, and he was on a collision course with Royce.

She had to stop it.

Sophie hurried to the door ahead of Royce and unlocked it so she could let in her father and Stanton. Her father immediately pulled her into his arms.

"Are you all right?" he asked. "Were you hurt?" Before Sophie could answer, he eased back and examined her face.

"I'm okay," she assured him.

She was far from okay, but her father was already worried enough without her adding the details of the attack. Still, it would take her a lifetime or two before she stopped hearing the sounds of those bullets and how close they'd come to killing Royce and her.

Her father let go of her, and with his hand extended, he made his way to Royce. "Thank you for saving her."

Royce had his gun in one hand, Travis's in the other so he didn't return the handshake. Didn't look too friendly, either. Probably because of Travis's accusation about her brother and father. An accusation that had to be a lie.

It just had to be.

Stanton had an equally bristled expression on his face. "What exactly happened?" he asked her.

Sophie decided to keep it short and sweet. "Travis and I broke up last night. This morning, an FBI agent called to warn me that someone was going to kidnap me. I ran, and Royce stopped two armed men from taking me. And from killing me," she added in a mumble.

Royce tipped his head to Travis. "He says you know something about those gunmen."

"He doesn't," Sophie argued.

But her father didn't exactly jump to agree with her. In fact, he shook his head and blindly fumbled behind him until he located the chair next to Maggie's desk. He practically dropped down onto the seat.

Oh, God.

Sophie started to go to him, but Royce latched on to her arm and held her back. "Just listen to what he has to say," Royce advised her.

Sophie didn't want to listen, and she didn't want her father to blurt out anything incriminating about those papers she'd found. Royce would have to arrest him then. Besides, she couldn't believe her father actually had anything to do with this.

When her father just sat there, shaking his head, Sophie looked at Stanton for some kind of explanation.

"I don't know what's going on," her brother muttered. But it seemed as if he did know *something.*

Sophie silently cursed. Stanton and she hadn't been close, not since her mother, Diane, had died a year ago in a car accident and had cut Stanton out of the will. Of course, maybe Stanton hadn't been expecting anything since he was Diane's stepson, but he darn well should have expected it since Diane had helped raise him. Stanton had only been five years old when Diane and Eldon had gotten married, and for all and intents and purposes, she'd been his mother.

Sophie returned her attention to her father—someone else her mother hadn't included in her will. She cursed that will now.

And her mother.

Because Diane had ripped the family apart by leaving Sophie everything and then forbidding her to give her father and brother a penny.

Her father finally looked up but not at her. At Royce. "I made some bad investments, and I used the ranch and land as collateral. I was on the verge of losing everything so I got a loan from someone. The *wrong someone*," he confessed.

"A loan shark?" Royce asked.

Eldon nodded, and her mouth went dry. *Mercy.* This was worse than she'd thought.

Royce turned to her, his eyebrow already lifted. "Did you know?"

It took her a moment before Sophie could speak and tamp down some of the wild ideas flying through her head. Or maybe not so wild. After all, a loan shark and the attack could be connected.

"I knew about the debts," she said. "But not about this extra *loan*."

"That's why Sophie was marrying Travis," Stanton added. "So he'd pay off all our father's debt, including the most recent one."

Sophie's gaze flew to Travis. "You knew about the loan shark?"

He lifted his shoulder. "Not specifically. I just knew your father was in financial hot water."

"And Travis wouldn't give us the money in advance," Stanton volunteered. "He insisted we wait until after the wedding."

Another lift of his shoulder. "A deal's a deal, and the deal was for Sophie."

"Well, that's off now, isn't it?" Stanton snarled. "And this loan shark threatened to get his money one way or another."

Royce jumped right on that. "By kidnapping Sophie?"

The room went completely silent for several long moments. The silence didn't help steady her nerves, that's for sure. Neither did her father's dire expression.

"Maybe," her father finally admitted.

She wanted to scream and pound her fists against the wall. How the heck had her father's finances come to this? And why had he kept something this important from her?

Sophie went to her father, latched on to his chin and forced eye contact. "Did this loan shark actually threaten to come after me?"

Her father didn't answer. Didn't have to. She saw it in his eyes.

"I'm sorry," he said, his voice a hoarse whisper. "He didn't threaten you specifically, but he said I'd be sorry if I didn't pay up. I thought he'd send one of his goons after me." Her father shook his head, groaned. "I didn't know he'd go after one of my kids."

Sophie backed away, and she hadn't realized that she was wobbling until she felt Royce take her arm to steady her.

"I should be the one comforting Sophie," Travis said, and he went to her as well and caught onto her other arm. "I think you and the cowboy can see now that I didn't have any part in the attack."

Sophie couldn't argue with that last part, but she shook off Travis's grip. After everything that had happened, it turned her stomach to have him touch her.

"As far as I'm concerned," Travis continued, "you're still my fiancée, and the wedding is still on. Once we've said our I do's, your father will have the money to pay off the loan shark and his other debts. The threat to your life will stop."

Everyone turned to her. She saw the hope in her father's eyes. The smugness in Travis's. Her brother just looked disgusted by the whole situation, but some of that disgust might be aimed at her since she hadn't been able to find a way around the terms of her mother's will.

But it was Royce's reaction that grabbed her attention.

He was staring at her, waiting, and he seemed

to be reminding her of that slap that Travis had given her. Sophie didn't need his reminder, because she could still feel the sting on her cheek. However, she wasn't sure she could let her father face down a loan shark, either.

Royce huffed, as if he knew exactly what she was thinking. "You don't have to marry a jackass to stop a criminal. That's what cops are for." He took a pen and paper from Maggie's desk and pushed it toward her father. "I want the name of the loan shark and any contact information you have."

Her father nodded. "His name is Teddy Bonner, and he's in Amarillo."

"This guy is clearly dangerous," Travis pointed out. "And besides, you're a small-town deputy sheriff. You hardly have the credentials to stop a loan shark."

Royce didn't glare. Just the opposite. He returned the smug expression. "I have a gun and a badge. Pretty good credentials if you ask me. And then there's the whole part about Sophie being here and not in the hands of the kidnapper. I'm pretty sure that means this small-town deputy outsmarted the dangerous loan shark."

Travis's eyes narrowed. "For now."

Royce leaned in. *"For now* is a good start. I plan to keep it that way."

Sophie wanted to cheer. Well, for a few seconds anyway. But then she remembered Royce was paying a very high price for her safety, and after what she'd done to him, she didn't deserve his help.

Her father wrote on the paper, handed it to Royce and then stood. "You'll stop this monster from going after Sophie?"

"I'll do my best," Royce promised.

"Are we free to go then?" Stanton asked.

Her brother was already turning toward the door when Royce answered, "No. Mr. Congeniality here," Royce continued, glancing at Travis, "said he had some photos sent to him anonymously. Know anything about that?" And, with another glance, Royce extended that question to her father.

"What photos?" her father immediately asked.

"Of Royce and me," she clarified when Royce hesitated. Maybe because he didn't want to have to explain anything about the incident in the motel. She certainly wasn't looking forward to explaining it, either, but it might be connected to the attack.

Her father's gaze flew to Travis. "What photos?" he repeated.

"Doctored ones, no doubt," Travis answered. "Unfortunately, I didn't realize that at the time, and it caused Sophie and me to have a little disagreement."

"He slapped her," Royce quickly provided, causing Travis's scowl to return.

"A small fit of temper, that's all," Travis growled. "It won't happen again."

Royce made a sound to indicate he wasn't buying that and looked at her brother again. "What do you know about those photos?"

"Nothing." Stanton dodged Sophie's and Royce's gazes, and he opened the door. "Time to go, Dad."

Her father hugged her and brushed a kiss on her cheek. "I'm so sorry," he whispered. "For everything."

The *for everything* made her freeze, and Sophie wanted to know what he meant by that. The engagement, maybe? But she didn't have time to ask, because Stanton took their father's arm and started to leave.

However, Eldon stopped and turned back to Royce. "This seems minor in light of what happened to Sophie and you, but someone broke into our house."

"When?" Royce and Sophie asked at the same time.

Eldon shook his head. "This morning. Maybe it was the gunmen looking for Sophie."

No doubt. They would have definitely searched the house for her.

"Anything missing?" Royce pressed.

Again, her father shook his head. "Not from what I can tell, but there was some furniture overturned and things out of place."

"I'd take some security precautions if I were you," Royce said. "In case those men return."

That got her moving, and Sophie raced toward the door where her father and brother were exiting. "Be careful."

"We will," Stanton assured her, and he practically stuffed Eldon into the car.

"Did you see the look on Stanton's face?" Travis remarked. "He doctored those photos so it'd break up you and me."

It was so ridiculous that she nearly laughed. "And why would he do something like that?" Sophie fired back. "Because without your money, my father loses the ranch and everything else. That means my brother loses, too."

His smug look returned. "You think Stanton cares about the ranch when he can get his hands on all that money your mother left you?"

She shook her head. "The only way Stanton could get the money is if I'm dead."

And it chilled her to the bone just to say that.

Travis shrugged. "You just spelled out your brother's motive. I figure he doctored those photos. Or maybe drugged you and the cowboy so he could get you in a compromising position. And then he sent the pictures to me, figuring I'd lose my temper and kill you. Or else hire some-one to do it."

Sophie wanted to deny all of that, but her throat clamped shut.

Oh, God.

Had Stanton done that?

"Here's another theory," Royce said. He moved closer, right by her side, so that their arms were touching, and they were facing Travis head-on. "You found out that Sophie and I had been *to-gether*, and you decided a slap wasn't enough punishment. You hired those men to kidnap her. Or kill her."

"I wouldn't do that," Travis argued.

"And then you come here, pretending that you're as innocent as a newborn calf," Royce continued, obviously ignoring Travis's remark.

He shook his head. "I'm not buying it."

"You don't have to *buy it*," Travis fired back. "Sophie's opinion is the only one that matters right now."

Both of them looked at her. Waiting. She'd just had an avalanche of information come at her, and she didn't know where to start sorting it all out. One thing was for certain—she trusted Royce.

Well, trusted him to keep her safe anyway.

Travis definitely didn't care for her hesitation. He huffed. "Sophie, here's the bottom line. If you don't leave with me now, the marriage is off, and your father loses everything. Maybe even his life." He looked at his watch. "You've got two minutes to decide."

Chapter Six

Royce didn't realize he was holding his breath until his lungs began to ache. Hell. He wanted to toss both Travis and his ultimatum out the door, but there was a lot at stake here.

For Sophie.

And for her family.

Travis might indeed save her father from going under financially, but Royce didn't trust the man. He wanted to believe it had nothing to do with Sophie herself. And especially nothing to do with their scalding-hot kissing session the month before. But he figured that his breath-holding wasn't a good sign.

"I'll check up on this loan shark," Royce told her as Travis kept his attention nailed to his watch. "If he sent those kidnappers after you, maybe I can prove it."

That would get the loan shark off the street, but it wouldn't pay off her father's debts. It also might not end the threats to Sophie and anyone else in her family.

"No," Sophie said. "Travis, I'm not going with you."

That was the answer Royce had hoped for, but he sure hadn't expected it. Maybe Sophie had realized just how dangerous Travis could be. Next time, the man might do more than just slap her.

"You know what's at stake," Travis warned her.

She nodded.

Travis waited several moments, maybe to see if she'd change her mind. When Sophie didn't budge, Travis cursed and headed for the door. "You're an idiot to trust that cowboy over me, and you'll be sorry."

Royce nearly gave a smart-mouthed reply, but the truth was, he wanted Travis out of there. He didn't have to wait long for that. Travis slammed the door and headed to his car across the street. Royce kept his eyes on him until the man had driven away.

Sophie was doing the same, and the moment he was out of sight, her breath swooshed out. "I've had more than enough excitement for one day," she mumbled. "I need to go home."

"You can't," Royce reminded her. "Those gunmen are still at large, and they could have your house under surveillance."

The color drained from her face. "I have to get out of here and go somewhere else then," she insisted.

Yeah. Royce knew how she felt. The adrenaline crash was no doubt hitting her pretty hard right now. Him, too. And now that the dust was settling, she was starting to realize just how close they'd come to dying today. Agent Lott was supposed to arrive soon, but they could reschedule their meeting with him. Sophie wasn't in any shape to face the questions he'd no doubt ask.

Her tears didn't return, thank God, but since she looked ready to keel over, he held her up. Sophie took the gesture one step further and leaned into him. Royce upped things too by looping his arm around her waist.

Then she sort of melted against him.

This holding was wrong, and Royce knew it. Sophie was business now. She was the target of hired guns, and that made her someone in his protective custody. Hugging her wasn't exactly crossing the line, but whenever he was close to her like this, his thoughts didn't stay just on hugging. Royce didn't remember everything that happened in the motel, but he sure as hell remembered kissing her.

And touching her.

There was even a blink of an image of him

unhooking her black lace bra and having her breasts spill out into his hands.

This wasn't a good time to relive that specific image. Not with her this close and not with Royce dealing with his own adrenaline crash.

"I need to get out of here," she repeated. She stayed melted against his body, and that didn't help clear Royce's head.

"We can go to my place," he heard himself offer.

She looked relieved, as if she wanted to jump at the idea. Royce wasn't jumping, that's for sure. It was a dangerous mix—them, alone at his place. But with this heat simmering between them, maybe there was no place safe. At least he had a security system at his house and the ranch hands could help him keep an eye out for the gunmen. So he rationalized that Sophie would be safer there.

Well, safer from gunmen anyway.

But maybe not from him.

"But what about the office?" she asked. "No one else is here."

"Give me a second." Royce called Billy and asked him to come in.

The deputy said he'd be there in ten minutes, but Royce didn't want to wait. He made a second call to one of the ranch hands, Tommy Rester, and asked him to secure the ranch.

Royce locked up Travis's gun in his desk and stuffed the paper with the loan shark's name and number in his shirt pocket. He hung the Be Back Soon sign in the window that had the emergency contact number. That was the advantage of living in a small town—people didn't expect the sheriff's office to be manned 24/7 as long as someone was on call and responded to 9-1-1.

He locked up and got Sophie moving toward his truck. The snow was light but still coming down, and the icy wind whipped at them. Royce got Sophie inside as quickly as he could, and on the drive to the ranch, he called Sergeant Frank Coulter, a cop in the Amarillo P.D.

Royce didn't put the call on Speaker, even though Sophie no doubt wanted to hear what the sergeant had to say. Still, she might need a toned down version though he had no idea how to tone down the fact that her father might have nearly gotten her killed.

"What do you know about a loan shark named Teddy Bonner?" Royce asked Frank.

"Plenty. Please don't tell me he's in Mustang Ridge."

"Maybe. Or maybe he just hired two goons to come after a local woman. When I intervened, they tried to gun down both of us."

The sergeant made a slight sound of surprise.

"You're sure it was Bonner behind that?"

"No, but the woman's father owes Bonner plenty of money." Royce glanced at Sophie, and she was leaning closer, trying to listen.

"The hired guns don't sound like Bonner," Frank continued. "Neither does the part about going for the guy's daughter. He's real old-school, Royce. Breaking kneecaps is more his style, and he hires muscle to do that. And I've never heard of him using family to get back at someone who owes him money."

Hell. If Bonner wasn't responsible for this, then they were right back to Travis.

"I can bring Bonner in and ask him a few questions," Frank offered. "Who's the fool stupid enough to borrow money from a worm like him?"

"Eldon Conway," Royce answered. "When I get the report done on the shooting, I'll send you a copy. There might be some details of the attack that we might be able to tie back to Bonner."

Royce thanked the sergeant, hung up.

"I heard," Sophie said.

Unlike him, she was no doubt relieved that her father's loan shark might not be the reason she'd nearly died. If it had been Bonner, it would have made this investigation a whole lot easier because he would have had an instant suspect and perhaps even a quick arrest.

Royce turned onto the ranch road, the tires

of his truck crunching over the snow and ice. Maybe the weather would slow down the gunmen enough for the Rangers to find them. Maybe. But Royce was guessing the pair already had an escape route planned before they even fired the first shot.

He spotted one of the ranch hands in the doorway of the barn nearest the front of the property. The hand was armed with a rifle. So was the one sitting in a truck by the cattle gate that stretched across the entire road. The moment that Royce drove through, the hand shut the gate.

"You have Angus cows," Sophie mumbled. "I wasn't sure what kind of livestock you raised."

Royce followed her gaze to the cows in the fenced pasture. They were indeed Angus, and since her father didn't raise cattle, only quarter horses, he was surprised she even recognized the breed.

"We have some Charolais, too," Royce explained.

Her attention went from the cows, to the outbuildings and then to the two-story ranch house where his father and sister, Nell, lived. Jake, Maggie and his niece, Sunny, were there, too, for now, but in another month or so they'd be moving to their own house that Jake was having built near the creek.

"It's a big place," she commented.

"Not as big as your father's. And we won't be staying here anyway. We'll be at my house, and it's a lot smaller than this place or yours," he clarified. "It's about a quarter of a mile from here."

"My father has land and the house, not me," she said a moment later. "But he had to sell the livestock because of his money problems."

Yeah. Royce had heard that. And that brought him to something he should probably let lie, but Eldon's money problems were perhaps connected to Sophie's safety. "Why doesn't he sell the ranch and pay off that loan shark?" Instead of trying to marry off Sophie to Travis.

She shook her head. "Even if he got top dollar for the place, it wouldn't be enough, and the ranch isn't worth what it was a few years ago."

Royce had to replay that in his head to make sure he'd heard her correctly. Maybe the value had gone down, but Eldon still had a lot of land. "How much does your father owe?"

"Honestly, I'm not sure, but from what I can tell he owes about a dozen people close to a million dollars. I don't know exactly how much of that has to be paid to Bonner."

Hell. "That was a lot of cash for Travis to cough up to marry you."

She made a sound of agreement. "But there's a twist," Sophie said as Royce came to a stop in front of his small, wood frame house. "My mother left me nearly ten million, and while there are a dozen or more conditions of her will that prevent me from giving money to my father and brother, there's nothing that prevents my spouse from dipping into it."

"Isn't that what prenups are for?" he immediately asked.

"Travis refused to sign one."

He thought about that. And cursed. "Then Travis could be pressing for this marriage so he can get his hands on your money?"

"Maybe. He said he wouldn't sign a prenup because he has triple the money that I do and doesn't need my inheritance, but I found some things in the papers I sent to Agent Lott that contradicts that. I believe Travis has the million to pay off my father's debts, but I think it would also wipe out his liquid assets."

"Yet you agreed to marry him? Hell's bells, Sophie," Travis could have been planning to kill you—" And his argument came to a halt. "But after the wedding. That's the only way he could have gotten his hands on your money."

She nodded.

"Travis could have sent the kidnappers, though," Royce added.

Another nod. "Maybe he was going to force me into the marriage. Or he's sick enough to stage my rescue so that I'd go running into his arms." She paused, shuddered. "But those men fired shots at us."

"Maybe not on Travis's orders," Royce had to admit. "They could have panicked or even thought they could scare us into surrendering."

Movement in the side mirror caught his eye, and Royce automatically went for his gun. He stopped, though, when he saw his father's truck coming up the road. Royce cursed. He didn't need this today.

"Trouble?" Sophie asked.

"Always," Royce mumbled.

He got out, Sophie did the same, and they went onto his porch, which was scabbed with ice. Sophie's left foot slipped, sliding her right back into Royce's arms, and that's when Chet stepped from his truck.

"Jake told me about the shooting," Chet greeted in his usual snarling tone. "Is that why you brought *her* here?"

Royce opened the door to his house and helped Sophie inside. It was not only warmer there, but it would get them out of the slipping embrace that his father had no doubt noticed.

"Sophie's in danger," Royce informed his father. "And yeah, that's why I brought her here."

Royce braced himself for a scathing reminder of that danger following her to the ranch. Chet had had a few run-ins with Eldon, so Royce figured his father would want her anywhere but there.

Of course, Chet felt that way about most people.

"I've heard talk," Chet said, his attention landing not on Royce but Sophie, "that my son might have gotten you pregnant."

Sophie made a sound of pure surprise, and if Chet's revelation hadn't stunned Royce for several seconds, he might have made that sound, too.

"Where did you hear that?" Royce demanded. "Around. Is it true?"

"No," Sophie insisted before Royce could tell Chet to mind his own business.

"Good." But there was no relief in Chet's weathered eyes when he looked at Royce. "I didn't think you were that stupid. Best to keep your jeans zipped around her sort."

Royce glanced at Sophie and saw the color rise in her cheeks. What Royce was feeling wasn't embarrassment. It was pure anger.

"*Her sort?*" Royce repeated. He eased Sophie back so he could step inside and meet his father's gaze. "What? You afraid I'll follow in your footsteps?"

Royce didn't give Chet a chance to answer. He'd made his point, and that point was for his father to back way off, especially when it came to Sophie.

He shut the door. And locked it. While he was at it, Royce set the security system. From the window, he saw his father mumble something and then get back in his truck and drive away. *Good.* He could only take Chet in small doses, and that had been a big enough dose to last him for weeks.

"Your father and you don't get along," Sophie commented. She took off her coat and put it on the peg next to the door.

"No one gets along with Chet." Royce shrugged.

"Well, except my three-year-old niece, Sunny. He doesn't bark and growl at her."

"Then there must be some good underneath that gruff exterior."

Royce took off his coat as well and put it over Sophie's. "If there is, I haven't found it yet. He definitely wouldn't offer me a hug like your old man did you back at the sheriff's office."

"Yes," she said softly. "He loves me. I just wish he were more responsible." She paused. "How do you think your father found out about the pregnancy lie?"

He huffed, tried to rub away his headache. "I don't know, and we won't get the answer from Chet until he's good and ready to spill it. But my guess is that Travis asked around to find out if we were seeing each other. Those kinds of questions wouldn't stay secret long in a small town."

There was also the possibility that someone had seen Sophie and him at the party and had started a rumor about a one-night stand. It wouldn't have been much of a leap to go from that to a pregnancy.

Yeah. That'd be a tasty bit of gossip.

"What was all that 'following in your footsteps' about?" she asked.

Royce didn't huff again, but he wanted to groan. He was hoping Sophie wouldn't mention that, and he was sorry he'd let his temper get the best of him. About that, anyway.

"My mom got pregnant before she and my dad were married. In fact, that's why they got married. Chet had gotten her pregnant and her father forced a shotgun wedding. Mother was a city girl, not at all happy living on a ranch. And even before she got cancer, she was miserable and unhappy."

"I'm sorry." Sophie reached out and touched his arm.

Royce wasn't exactly comfortable with the sympathy. "Your parents don't appear to have had a good marriage, either."

"No," she agreed. "They divorced when I was seven. My mother got full custody of me, and we moved to Chicago. I had to beg her just to see my father and brother."

Well, Royce sure hadn't known that. "I thought you stayed away by choice."

She lifted her shoulder. "Sometimes I did. It was easier than arguing with my mother, something we always did when I wanted to see my dad. And after college, my life and job were in Chicago so I had even more reasons to stay away."

"You ran your mother's charity foundation," he remarked. "Still do."

Sophie blinked as if surprised he'd known that. Royce was surprised, too, but when it came to Sophie, little details about her just seemed to stick in his head. He blamed that on the attraction, but the truth was, he'd found her interesting—in an "opposites attract" sort of way.

"I remember when you moved back here last year," he said. Yeah, definitely opposites, but that hadn't stopped him from noticing her.

"I remember, too. Stanton introduced us at a get-together at the Millers'?" She eased her hand from his arm. No longer touching him. "You hated me. Maybe still do."

Royce opened his mouth to deny that.

"I heard you call me Prissy Pants, among other things," she added. "And you made your disapproval crystal clear."

Royce couldn't deny that. He had. "I tend to steer clear of women who aren't comfortable in jeans and boots." He groaned at the sound of that. "Except you look pretty darn comfortable in those jeans."

Hot, too.

Royce especially didn't want to voice that.

Her mouth trembled a little as if threatening to smile. But no smile came. However, she touched him again. Well, not him exactly, but when she scrubbed her hands up and down her arms, she brushed against his sleeve.

"So, you didn't hate me. You hated my clothes," she commented.

Now Royce felt himself smile. And God knows why, because he didn't have anything to smile about. He had a hundred things he should be doing instead of standing there while Sophie sort of touched him. Still, it felt good not to see the fear and worry in her eyes.

Oh, man.

He had that thought a moment too soon because when she looked up at him, the worry was back.

"I've dragged you into a bad mess," she whispered.

He heard the apology coming on, and he didn't want to listen to it. Royce didn't want that worry on her face, either. And for reasons he really didn't care to explore, he didn't want her stepping away from him. He caught onto her arm when she started to move away, and he eased her back to him.

Another hug.

Yet more touching that he shouldn't be doing.

But judging from the way she pulled in her breath, she needed it. What she didn't need was any other contact with him. Definitely no kissing.

But then Sophie looked up at him at the exact moment that Royce looked down at her.

Their breath met.

The front of her body brushed against his.

And his brain turned to dust.

Royce made things worse by lowering his head, but Sophie lifted hers. Meeting him in the middle. And they met all right.

Mouth to mouth.

This time, the sound she made wasn't one of relief. Nope. That little hitching sound of pleasure went through him like liquid fire because in that sound he heard the need. The heat—and worse, worse, the surrender.

Hell.

One of them needed to stay sane here, and surrendering wasn't a good way to do that.

But the insanity didn't stop with just a touch of their lips. Despite the lecture he was giving himself, Royce's hand went around to the back of her neck, and he snapped her to him. Sophie did some snapping of her own by sliding her arms around his waist. And just like that, the kiss became openmouthed. Hungry.

And very dangerous.

He remembered that taste. One of the few things he did remember about kissing her at the Outlaw Bar. It made his body want more, more, more. So, Royce took more. He deepened the kiss. Pressed harder against her. Until his body wanted more than *more*.

His body wanted sex with Sophie.

Thank goodness they had to break for air because in that split second when they were gulping in breaths, Royce forced himself to remember that this wasn't just a bad idea, it was crossing a legal line that shouldn't be crossed.

He let go of her. Not easily. But he eased back his hands and stepped away.

Sophie didn't come after him. Good thing, too, or he would have been toast. Instead, she stood there, breathing hard and looking very confused about what had just happened.

She mumbled some profanity. "We don't need this."

Royce couldn't have agreed more. But that didn't do much to cool the heat inside him. In fact, he was already thinking about what it would be like to be with her again. And this time, he would remember, unlike their encounter at the Outlaw Bar.

The sound shot through the room, and because Royce was still fighting the effects of that stupid kiss, it took him a moment to realize it was just his phone ringing. He took the cell from his jeans pocket and saw that the caller was Tommy Rester, one of the ranch hands. Since Tommy was in charge of setting up security, Royce quickly answered it.

"We got a visitor," Tommy greeted. "Special Agent Keith Lott from the FBI. I made him show me his badge, and it looks real."

Because it probably was. "Where is he?"

"At the gate. He said he went by the sheriff's office in town but that Billy told him you'd already left. Billy wouldn't say where you'd gone, but I guess Lott figured you might be here. I didn't confirm that, though."

Good. "Did Agent Lott say what he wanted?"

"Oh, yeah. And he didn't mince his words. He said he was here to find Sophie Conway and that if we didn't tell him where she was, he'd arrest us all on the spot."

Royce tried not to let his temper get in on this. Lott might be just concerned about Sophie, that's all. And with good reason after that attack. Heck, the agent might believe he was holding Sophie against her will since Sophie herself had thought that Royce might want to do her harm.

"Agent Lott is here?" Sophie asked.

Royce nodded, and he moved closer to Sophie so she could hear what Tommy was saying. He had to decide how to handle this. But really there was only one thing he could do. He had to see the agent and hope that Lott could help him stop the person behind the attack. Also, Lott might be able to fill him in on the FBI investigation that had started all of this in the first place.

"Bring Lott to my house," Royce instructed.

"Will do. One more thing, though," Tommy added. "Agent Lott said he was here because this case wasn't in your jurisdiction and that he'd be putting Sophie into his protective custody. Royce, he's taking her to Amarillo, ASAP."

Chapter Seven

Because Sophie had stepped way back from Royce, she hadn't heard exactly what the caller said about Agent Lott, but judging from Royce's renewed scowl, it wasn't good. She tried to brace herself for another round of bad news and added a silent warning and reminder to herself that she should be focused on finding a way out of the danger.

Instead of kissing Royce.

Later, when her body had cooled down some, she might realize just how bad of a mistake that kiss had been. It had certainly broken down some walls between Royce and her, and it wasn't a good time for that to happen.

"Did they find the gunmen?" she asked. But Royce's scowl didn't offer much hope.

Royce shook his head and pocketed his phone.

"Lott wants to take you into protective custody."

Oh. That probably shouldn't have been a surprise. After all, she'd nearly been killed just a few hours earlier, but Sophie hadn't considered leaving Mustang Ridge.

Or Royce.

Yes, he was playing into her decision-making process as well, and he shouldn't. Besides, getting away from him was probably a good idea. It might even get him out of danger.

Might.

Without offering her an opinion on how he felt about protective custody or Lott's arrival, Royce disarmed the security system and opened the door. Just moments later, the black four-door car came to a stop in front of the house, and the bulky, blond-haired man got out. Ducking his head down against the wind, Agent Lott hurried onto the porch.

Sophie had met with the agent at least a half-dozen other times, usually at a coffee shop or café. Never in his office where someone might see her coming and going. And in those meetings he had worn jeans and casual shirts. He hadn't looked much like an agent.

Today, he did.

Lott wore a dark suit and mirrored shades. When the wind flipped back the side of his jacket, she saw the leather shoulder holster and the gun inside it. His badge was clipped onto his belt.

"Sophie," Lott greeted. He tugged off the shades and hooked them on the front of his shirt.

Royce stepped to the side so Lott could enter the house, and he checked around the grounds. Maybe to make sure Lott hadn't been followed. He finally closed the door several seconds later.

"I'm S.A. Keith Lott," he said, and Royce and he exchanged a handshake. "You must be Deputy McCall. I owe you a huge thanks for keeping Sophie safe."

"I was doing my job," Royce answered, and he sounded a little offended that the agent had thanked him.

"Are you okay?" Lott asked her.

She nodded. "You know what happened?"

"I got a full update from the Rangers. They didn't find the gunmen, but the FBI's trying to get a match on the blood taken from the woods." He spared Royce a glance. "We pulled the Rangers off the investigation. The locals, too."

That didn't improve Royce's expression. "I asked the Rangers to come to assist," Royce stated. "I didn't ask you to come, and I damn sure didn't give you permission to interfere in my investigation."

"I didn't need your permission," Lott said.

"How'd you figure that? The shooting happened within the Mustang Ridge jurisdiction."

Lott pulled back his shoulders. "Sophie is a protected witness in my investigation."

"But the shooting might not have had anything to do with that investigation," Royce countered. "I haven't determined that yet."

"Investigate all you want, but Sophie's coming with me." Lott latched on to her arm, and Sophie automatically threw off his grip. Maybe she was reacting to the bad day she'd had, but she didn't like this territorial attitude.

Lott looked as if she'd slapped him. "You're siding with this local yokel?"

Now it was her shoulders that came back, and she stepped in front of Royce. Sophie didn't think he'd actually punch the agent, but it was clear he was having to hold on to his temper.

Sophie, too.

She'd never seen Lott act this way, and she didn't like it. He was reminding her too much of Travis.

"Did you hear what Royce said?" she asked Lott. "This attack might not be related to Travis or the papers I've been copying for you."

It could all go back to the loan shark. Of course, Royce and she had already learned that this wasn't Teddy Bonner's usual way to deal with a delinquent payee, but perhaps Bonner had made an exception in her father's case.

"Maybe," Lott conceded, but he didn't sound

one bit convinced. "I'm working with two likeli-hoods, and one is that your ex-fiancé hired those men to kidnap you because he knows we're clos-ing in on him."

"You think Travis got suspicious?" Royce asked.

"It's possible. Heck, he might have even seen Sophie snooping around his office."

Sophie shook her head. "Travis said nothing to me about the investigation."

"But you told me you argued with him and broke things off," Lott said.

"Yes." She didn't want to discuss those alleged photos of Royce and her with Agent Lott. "The argument I had with him was, well, personal."

Lott stared at her, as if waiting for more, but she didn't give it to him.

Royce stepped to Sophie's side so he was fac-ing Lott. "What exactly did Travis do to make you go to Sophie and ask her to help?"

Lott paused so long that Sophie wasn't sure he was going to answer. "Basically, he's money laundering through land deals and using that money to buy illegal arms. Forgive me if I don't give you the specifics, but while Sophie obvi-ously trusts you, I don't."

"You think I'm dirty?" Royce asked.

Lott shrugged. "It's occurred to me that Travis had some help. Maybe from local law enforcement."

"Not from me." Royce leaned in. "And not from my brother."

Sophie agreed. Jake and Royce were taking huge risks to protect her, and there's no way Royce would help a man like Travis.

She silently groaned. Her objectivity was shot. And that wasn't a good sign. Obviously, that lecture she'd given herself earlier had failed bigtime.

Sophie blew out a weary breath. "You said there were *two* likelihoods," she reminded Lott. Maybe the second one wouldn't involve revealing compromising photos of her and Royce.

The agent hesitated, dodged her gaze. Definitely not a good sign.

"What?" Sophie pressed.

"Your father could have hired those men." Lott's attention whipped to Royce. "And before you say that makes it a local case, it doesn't. Sophie's father is under federal investigation, too."

It felt as if her heart skipped a beat. Royce no doubt knew what this was doing to her because he caught her arm to steady her.

"I didn't tell you," Lott said to her, his voice just barely above a whisper now. "I *couldn't*. But it's possible your father participated in some of those illegal land deals with Travis."

He had. Sophie had hidden the papers that would prove it, though. But she had no plans to admit that to Lott. So the agent had two likelihoods to explain the attack, and she was withholding possible evidence for both of them.

Mercy.

"Are you saying Sophie's father sent those kidnappers after her?" Royce asked.

"I'm saying it's possible."

"It's not," Sophie argued. She still trusted her father. Had to. Because she loved him. And that meant this had to go back to Travis.

Lott turned to her again. "I don't think your father tried to kill you. Not exactly, anyway. But he might have sent those kidnappers to force you to go through with the marriage."

That had already crossed her mind. But Sophie had dismissed it, too. Or rather she'd tried to do that. However, she couldn't dismiss the fact that her father was desperate.

"My father borrowed money from a loan shark," Sophie admitted.

Lott certainly didn't look surprised. In fact, he nodded. "Teddy Bonner. Yeah. He didn't hire those men, either. I wouldn't want this to get around, but Bonner's an FBI criminal informant. He might be responsible for an assault every now and then, but he's not a killer."

And that meshed with what the cop in Amarillo had said. Still, Sophie could hold out hope that the culprit was anyone but her father—even if it was related to something he'd done, like borrowing money from a loan shark.

"You're not stupid," Lott said to Sophie. "You must know I can do a better job protecting you than the deputy can. Plus, there's *his* safety to consider. He's already been under fire because of you. Now he's brought you, and therefore the danger, to his family's home."

It was true.

She had known that, of course, but it *was* a powerful reminder to hear it spoken aloud.

Lott reached for her hand, and this time Sophie didn't push him away. "We need to leave now," he insisted. "It's the safest thing for everyone."

"Maybe we should wait for a blood match on the gunman I shot," Royce interrupted. "His identity could connect us to the person who hired him."

"We might not get a match," Lott countered, dropping his grip on her hand.

Royce gave him a flat stare. "If he's a hired gun, he's probably in the system. Just knowing who he is could tell us a lot about him and maybe his associates, too."

"And while we're waiting on results, the danger doesn't stop for you or your family," Lott mumbled a profanity. "Sophie doesn't need your death on her hands."

Her heart was racing now. Breath, too. And she nodded in agreement. "I'll go with you." She looked up at Royce. "Think of your family," she added in a whisper.

"I have," Royce insisted. "And those gunmen might show up whether you're here or not. They know my name, and it wouldn't be hard to figure out where I live. That's why I took security measures by having the hands armed and on the lookout."

"But this ranch will never be as secure as an FBI safe house," Lott huffed. "Look, I know Sophie and you had a fling or something, and that's probably why you feel the need to interject yourself into this."

Sophie went still. "A fling?" she repeated at the same moment that Royce said, "Who told you that?"

She hadn't mentioned a word to Lott about her encounter with Royce at the Outlaw Bar.

Lott shoved his hands in his pockets, and he shook his head. "I can't say."

"You mean you won't," Royce accused. Every muscle in Lott's face tightened. "All right, *I won't.* I got the information from a confidential source."

"My brother?" she blurted out.

Lott didn't deny it, but she thought she saw something go through his eyes. A confirmation, maybe. *Mercy.* She really needed to have a talk with Stanton. If he'd sent those pictures to Travis, maybe he'd also told Lott.

But there was a problem with that theory.

Stanton didn't know about the investigation. Or if he did, he hadn't said anything about it. Was her brother in on the investigation, too? And if so, why hadn't he said a word about it to her?

"What did your informant tell you about the *fling?*" Royce asked, and he didn't ask nicely, either.

"He told me enough." And with that vague bit of information, Lott's narrowed gaze cut to Sophie. "I can't believe with everything going on, you had unprotected sex with this guy. If you'd just pretended to be the doting fiancée a little bit longer, we could have arrested Travis before he got suspicious."

Sophie wasn't sure what hit her the hardest— the surprise that Lott knew about the pregnancy lie, Lott's unprofessional attitude or that someone, this confidential source, had talked about her to a federal agent. She opened her mouth to explain to Lott that she wasn't pregnant, but Royce stepped in front of her.

"What happened between us is none of Lott's business," Royce assured her. "And it's damn sure not the business of this so-called confidential informant."

Sophie agreed with that, but she thought maybe Royce, too, would like to have her straighten out the lie she'd told. His father had already given him grief about it, and it was only a matter of time before it was all over town.

Or maybe it already was.

Even though it was an old-fashioned notion that Royce's reputation might be hurt, it was possible for that to happen in a small town like Mustang Ridge. After all, he was the deputy sheriff, and it might be harder to do his job if the more conservative residents thought he had drunken one-night stands.

"None of my business?" Lott repeated, punctuating with some profanity. He opened his mouth to say more, but his phone rang, cutting him off.

The agent answered the call but stepped away from them. Not that he could step away far. The front part of the house wasn't that large—a living room on one side, a dining area on the other. But to put some distance between them, Lott moved to the fireplace on the far side of the wall and turned his back to them. He also spoke in a whisper.

"You trust him?" Royce asked her, whispering as well. Sophie wanted to say yes. After all,

Lott was a federal agent, and she'd put herself and others in possible jeopardy by providing him with those incriminating papers about Travis's land deals. Still, there was something about him that she hadn't seen before today.

Desperation, maybe?

Perhaps he really just wanted Travis arrested and her safe, but Sophie suddenly didn't feel very safe with him. Just the opposite. She felt as if Lott was trying to bully her into doing what he wanted. That might or might not be the safest thing for her to do.

"I'd like to stay with you," she said, her offer tentative. "But I don't want to put you or your family in any more danger."

Royce shook his head. "My niece, Sunny, has some treatments starting first thing tomorrow morning at a hospital in Amarillo. Jake, Maggie and she'll be up there for a couple of days."

Yes, she remembered them talking about it at the sheriff's office. "But what about your sister, Nell, and your father?"

"Nell will go to the hospital with the others."

So all but his father would be away from the ranch. Away from her. Where they'd be a heck of a lot safer. Still, she didn't like the idea of Chet being in the possible line of fire. He'd already made it clear that he wasn't comfortable with her being there.

"Any chance your father will go to the hospital with the others?" she asked.

"Possibly." Royce lifted his shoulder. "Chet and Sunny are close, so he'll want to be there for at least part of the procedure." He stared at her. "My advice—don't insist he leave for safety's sake. He's a stubborn man, and that would make him only dig in his heels and stay put."

Sophie was afraid of that.

"Chet can take care of himself," Royce added. "Don't let any part of your decision be about him."

Hard to do that. Chet might not be likable, but she didn't want him hurt. But she remembered something else Royce had said. Even if she left, the gunmen might still come to the McCall ranch looking for her.

She hated that this was yet another situation of being between a rock and a hard place.

Lott finished his call and turned back toward them. "They found one of the gunmen, wounded but alive."

Sophie had braced herself for more bad news, but this was better than she'd expected. "Is he talking?"

Lott slipped on his mirrored shades and headed for the door. "That's what I'm about to find out." Royce reached for his coat. "We'll go with you."

"No." Lott didn't look back when he opened the door. "The gunman's in FBI custody, and they have orders not to let you near the place."

"Whose orders?" Royce challenged.

"*Mine.*" Lott glanced over his shoulder at Sophie. "Are you coming with me? I figured you'd want to find out why this guy tried to kidnap you."

Oh, she wanted to know that, but that little niggling feeling in the back of her head got worse. And Sophie hoped she wasn't about to make this decision—maybe the most important one of her life—because Royce's kisses had clouded her judgment.

However, Sophie decided to go with the niggling feeling about Lott. And with trusting Royce.

"I'm staying here," she said.

Because of the shades, she couldn't see the reaction in Lott's eyes, but his mouth certainly tightened. "Suit yourself," he grumbled. "And I hope to hell you don't get the deputy here killed."

Yes. Sophie was hoping the same thing.

But Sophie thought of something else. Another factor in her decision to stay here at Royce's house.

Royce himself and the heat between them.

Sophie looked at him and figured he was thinking the same thing. Just because she wanted the attraction to go away, it didn't mean it would. In fact, it was getting stronger. And she'd just agreed to stay under the same roof with the man she couldn't resist.

But a man she had to resist.

Their situation was already dangerous enough without adding more of this fire to the mix. Besides, the fire could also end up being a deadly distraction. Like her, Royce's attention needed to be on solving this case and making the danger go away. That wouldn't happen if the kissing started again.

And kissing wasn't even the worst of it.

She wanted him, bad, and she was afraid *that* need would overrule common sense. If she let it. The trick was to stop that from happening.

"I need to get some rest," she told Royce. Not a lie exactly. She was exhausted, but rest would give her more than just, well, rest.

He tipped his head to the room off the right of the kitchen. "The spare bedroom," he explained.

Sophie mumbled a thanks and she practically ran there and shut the door. She needed space and time to think. But most of all, she had to put—and keep—some distance between Royce and her.

Chapter Eight

Royce pressed the end call button on his phone and cursed. This was not the start to the day that he wanted. A double dose of bad news.

Triple, he corrected when he looked at the email that popped into the in-box on his laptop. The investigation hadn't just stalled, it was going backward.

He got up from the kitchen table where he'd been working and poured himself another cup of coffee. There'd likely be more cups, too, since he was nursing a wicked headache from the spent adrenaline and the lack of sleep. He'd caught a couple of hours' sleep. Catnaps, really. But that's all he'd been able to manage, what with listening for an attack and trying to figure out who wanted Sophie dead.

There was no shortage of suspects, either—Travis, Stanton, her father. Maybe even the loan shark Teddy Bonner. Royce didn't want to add

Agent Lott to that mental list, but he didn't trust the man.

With reason.

The second bit of bad news Royce had gotten confirmed his suspicions about the agent. Now, the question was—what was he going to do about it?

He automatically reached for his gun when he heard the hurried footsteps. It took Royce a split second to remember that he wasn't alone. And that he had a houseguest.

Sophie.

The main reason he hadn't slept well.

She hurried into the kitchen and came to a sliding stop on the tiled floor. She had on a pair of black socks and pajamas. *His* clothing items. The pj's practically swallowed her body, but somehow managed to skim her body, too.

Royce forced himself not to notice that.

"Sorry. I don't usually sleep this late." Sophie pushed her hair from her face, but it tumbled right back into a sexy heap that pooled on the tops of her shoulders. "You should have woke me up."

"No reason. You needed to rest." He took out another cup and poured her some coffee.

"But you've been working, and I should be helping you." She tipped her head to the laptop and made a sound of approval when she drank some of the coffee. "Any updates on the investigation?"

Royce had hoped she wouldn't ask about that until at least she'd had her coffee, because she might need a clear head to process everything he needed to tell her—especially since it was all bad. He decided to start with the easiest item of bad news, but then stopped when he saw the SUV drive away from the main ranch house.

Sophie hurried to the window, her gaze following his. "Your brother?" she asked.

He nodded. "Nell, Maggie and he are leaving for Sunny's appointment at the hospital."

And that meant Jake was unable to help with the investigation. Not that Royce wanted Jake here, because his brother already had enough to keep him busy. Still, Royce wouldn't have minded having another pair of eyes and ears on the information he'd just learned.

"You said they wouldn't be back for several days?" Sophie moved next to him, her arm against his. A reminder of the day before. A reminder of the kiss, too.

Royce didn't move. He stood there, knowing full well that it wasn't a good idea to be this close to Sophie. She had bedroom hair, bedroom eyes and a mouth he wanted in his bedroom. The rest of her, too.

"That's right," he answered.

"Days," she repeated in a mumble, and she slid her gaze over their touching arms and to his face.

Yes, as in days Sophie and he would be alone. Well, except for his father and the ranch hands. Maybe her brother, too. Stanton had already called twice and requested a visit. So perhaps their alone time wouldn't be so alone after all.

Royce tried to remind himself that was a good thing.

Of course, the weather could work against them, as well. The second wave of the snowstorm was moving in, and it might be worse than the first. Sophie and he didn't need the weather trapping them, just in case he decided to move her elsewhere.

Or in case he needed a break from her and all those bedroom reminders.

"Amarillo P.D. questioned the loan shark Teddy Bonner," Royce said, forcing his mind back on his triple bad news he had to tell her. "They found no evidence that he was connected to the attack on us."

Sophie blew out a long breath, and he heard the frustration in that simple gesture. Yeah, this would have been so much easier if Bonner had been the culprit because the loan shark could have been arrested and off the street. Of course, Sophie would have still had to contend with Travis, but that would be much easier if he wasn't a would-be kidnapper or killer.

"Lott was right about Bonner being a criminal informant. Amarillo P.D. doesn't use him often, but they've found him 'reliable in certain situations.'" That was the cop's exact wording. Which was no doubt code for Bonner being a snitch to help Amarillo P.D. nab someone much worse than the loan shark himself.

"What about the wounded gunman?" she continued. "Did Lott get anything from him?"

Here was the second dose of bad news. "The guy died before Lott could even question him."

No long breath this time. She groaned.

"They did get an ID with his fingerprints," Royce explained. Which could have potentially been good news if he'd lived and hadn't had such a long criminal past. "He was a low-life thug who's worked for a lot of people over the years. *A lot*," he emphasized.

"But not Travis?" she pressed.

Royce shook his head. "There's no obvious connection to Travis." Nor to any of their other suspects except for her father, and Royce figured Eldon wasn't even on Sophie's suspect list. However, her father was on Royce's.

"We'll keep looking for a money trail," Royce continued. "Someone paid him to attack you, and there'll be a record of it." *Maybe.* "Plus, we might catch the second gunman."

Sophie didn't look very hopeful about that. With reason. It'd been twenty-four hours since the attack, and the guy could be out of the country by now.

Of course, that was better than the alternative. That the gunman was nearby and planning to come after them again.

Royce glanced out of the corner of his eye and realized she was studying him. "Something else is wrong," Sophie concluded.

Bingo. And it was this something else that troubled him more than the other bad news he'd already delivered to her.

"I have a friend in the FBI, Kade Ryland. And I called him yesterday and asked him to quietly look at Lott's investigation into Travis's criminal activity." He paused. "There is no official investigation."

Sophie blinked. "Maybe it's classified or something?"

"Ryland has the authority to check for that sort of thing." He turned so they were facing each other. "In fact, there weren't even any flags or files on Travis that would have triggered a federal investigation."

"But Travis was doing illegal stuff," she quickly pointed out. "I saw the papers for two illegal land deals, and I copied them and gave them to Lott."

Now here's where things could get sticky. "Did Lott ever say why he suspected Travis of those deals?"

Sophie hesitated again before she shook her head. "Lott only said that Travis was under investigation and that he was a dangerous man. I think it was the dangerous part that convinced me to get those papers. I sensed something was wrong, that Travis couldn't be trusted, so I wanted to see what he was up to."

"And you were maybe looking for a way out of the engagement?" Royce asked.

"That, too." She groaned softly and stepped away from him. "I knew marrying him would help my father, but I didn't trust Travis. I wasn't sure he'd actually pay my father the money if I went through with the marriage."

And he might not have. The marriage might have been Travis's way of getting his hands on Sophie's money. "You were right not to trust him."

"But maybe wrong to trust Lott," Sophie finished for him.

There it was in a nutshell. Lott's unauthorized investigation was bad news number three, but Royce didn't know just what level of bad it was. Maybe Lott was a dirty agent. Or maybe he had someway found out about Travis's illegal activity and had bent some big rules to go after him. Either way, the agent had put Sophie in danger, and in Royce's book, that made Lott *bad*.

"So what do we do about Lott?" she asked.

"We don't trust him." That was the obvious part. The next would take a little time, and during that time, they'd just have to do their best to avoid Lott. "Agent Ryland is going to do some more checking and talk with Lott's supervisor."

"Lott won't like that," she mumbled.

No. And Royce was sure he'd hear from the agent as soon as he found out that Royce had gone behind his back to get answers about the investigation.

"Good thing I didn't leave with Lott yesterday when he was here," Sophie added.

Royce shrugged. "It's hard to argue with that, but I can see why a peace officer would want to stop a guy like Travis. Hell, I want to beat him to a pulp for hitting you."

Sophie's hand went to her cheek, and he could tell she was reliving that particular bad memory. "You were right. I should have filed charges against him for assault."

"It's not too late. Maybe we can tack it on to the other charges against him."

Before the last word left his mouth, his phone rang. Royce put his coffee aside and looked at the screen, bracing himself for more bad news. And maybe it was. Stanton's name was there, and Royce showed her the screen before he answered the call on Speaker.

"Royce," Stanton immediately said. "Where's Sophie? I need to speak to her."

Royce looked at her to see if she wanted to respond. She huffed softly and moved closer to the phone. "Stanton, is something wrong?" she asked.

He didn't answer right away, and that tightened Royce's stomach. "I have to tell you some things," Stanton finally said.

"I'm listening," Sophie assured him.

"I can't talk about this over the phone. I need to see you. You need to know what I did."

The tightening in Royce's stomach turned to a big knot. "What'd you do, Stanton?" he demanded.

"I'll tell you when I see Sophie."

Royce figured that wasn't the best option here.

"It's not safe for Sophie to be out and about. If you're worried about someone eavesdropping, then call me back on my landline."

"No. This has to be done face-to-face. Can you meet me at the sheriff's office in two hours?"

Royce checked his watch, though time wasn't the issue. Sophie's safety was. "You're positive this is worth risking your sister's life?"

Stanton cursed. "What I have to tell you might be the reason Sophie's in danger. So you decide. If it's worth the risk, be at the sheriff's office."

And with that, Stanton hung up.

"Any idea what that's about?" Royce asked her as he put his phone back in his pocket.

"The pictures, maybe?" Sophie didn't hesitate, either. "Travis seemed to believe that Stanton had something to do with that."

Maybe he did. After all, Stanton had been at the Outlaw Bar that night. But Royce couldn't see how that would be so critical that Stanton had to tell Sophie in person. Maybe it was something more. Something that pertained to the investigation.

Or it could be a trap.

Royce hated to think that, but Sophie's brother could want her dead so that Eldon and he could inherit all the money. Sophie was worth millions, more than enough to pay off Eldon's debts and get the Conway ranch back on track. People had killed for a lot less, and if Stanton was as devoted to Eldon as Sophie was, he might be willing to sacrifice his sister for their father.

Yeah. This could definitely be a trap.

"I don't think it's a good idea for us to meet him," Royce let her know.

The surprise flashed through Sophie's eyes, and she opened her mouth. No doubt to defend

Stanton as she'd been doing with her father. But she closed her mouth and stared at him.

"It's too risky," she whispered, and it wasn't exactly a question.

Royce made a sound of agreement. "If it's as important as Stanton seems to think it is, we'll make other arrangements to hear what he has to say. A video call, maybe. But I really don't want you leaving the house and going into town where you could easily be spotted by someone."

Like the surviving gunman.

She nodded, eased her cup to the table and leaned her head against the window. "I don't want to believe my brother would harm me."

Royce understood. "He's not our primary suspect," he reminded her.

But Stanton *was* a suspect.

And Sophie's heavy sigh let him know that she was well aware of that. Good. At least she was starting to see her brother through a cop's eyes. Maybe soon she'd do the same for her father. Royce wasn't convinced there was a solid reason to distrust either Stanton or Eldon, but until he knew who was behind the attack, he didn't want to take any unnecessary risks.

She turned and eased right into his arms. Royce didn't back away. Just the opposite. And that caused huge alarms to go off in his head.

He ignored them.

Royce also ignored the lecture he'd been giving himself for the past twenty-four hours—the one that insisted he should avoid getting any closer to Sophie. Heck, he ignored everything he shouldn't ignore and brushed a kiss on her forehead.

She groaned softly, probably because she'd been telling herself the same thing—stay away. Run. Don't get too close. But since she didn't budge, it was clear her body was having the same stubborn reaction that his was.

"I've been trying to avoid this," she mumbled.

"Yeah. So have I." He was failing so badly that he might have to give *failure* a whole new name. Worse, he wanted to fail even harder.

She looked up at him, shook her head. "What are we going to do about this?"

Since the answer on the tip of his tongue was *have sex*, Royce didn't say it out loud. Though judging from the heated look she was giving him, maybe it was on the tip of her tongue, too.

He'd never really had a type of woman he preferred. Hair and eye color didn't matter, and he'd dated both thin and those with curves, but now looking down at Sophie, he knew he'd finally found his type. Maybe it was that tumbled hair. That face. Or those curves hidden in his clothes. Whatever it was, Sophie was it.

Man, he was toast.

Royce fought the urge to kiss her and felt himself losing that battle, too. "When this is over, maybe we can have dinner or something."

She blinked. "You mean like a date?"

"Exactly like a date." It seemed like a good place to start, anyway, and it was something he could put off until Sophie was no longer "the job."

Well. He could put it off if he kept his hands and mouth to himself. That was a big *if* since she was already in his arms.

"We seem a little past the first-date stage," she pointed out.

"We are." Especially after making out at the Outlaw Bar. "But I'm figuring we can backtrack." It seemed more sensible that going full steam ahead, something his body was encouraging him to do.

Sophie nodded hesitantly. "I'm not your type," she reminded him. "I'm a city girl, like your mother."

"Yeah," he settled for saying. "I didn't say a date was a good idea."

And neither was the kiss he pressed on her mouth.

It wasn't quite the same as having her for breakfast, but it felt like a good start. Even when Royce knew he shouldn't be starting anything sexual with her.

He pulled back, enjoying the nice little buzz of heat that went through the middle of his body. Royce enjoyed the flash of surprise in her eyes, too. Not from fear or hearing bad news. This was surprise of a sexual nature. Maybe Sophie had gotten a buzz, as well.

"Yes," she mumbled.

She moved away, nervously sliding her hands down the sides of the pajamas, and the motion stretched the thin fabric over her breasts. No bra. Because he could clearly see the outline of her nipples.

That buzz got stronger.

Royce felt his resolve get weaker. Of course, that always seemed to happen whenever he was around Sophie.

Yeah, she was his type, all right.

Their gazes met again. Held. There was a split second of time when Royce thought he could put a choke hold on the ache burning in his body. That split second came and went. And Royce moved toward her at the same time she moved toward him. It wasn't slow. Certainly not tentative. They moved like two people who seemed to know exactly what they were doing.

That couldn't have been further from the truth. This time, there was no restraint, no holding back. Willpower and common sense vanished, and Royce helped keep those things at bay when he hooked his arm around Sophie's waist and hauled her to him.

They collided—too crazy from the need to give this make-out session much finesse. But they adjusted, automatically, as if they'd done this so many times that they knew exactly how and where to move. Not a comforting thought.

The kiss was instant and hot. Openmouthed, hungry. It felt as if they were starved for each other and even as the sensations roared through him, a little voice inside Royce's head kept telling him this was a bad idea.

It was.

But that didn't stop him from pulling her body against his. He'd been right about that no bra part. Equally right about how she'd feel in his arms with her braless breasts pressed against his chest.

Sophie made a sound. Part moan, part shiver. She sort of melted against him, every part of her seemingly touching every part of him. Well, except one part that was suddenly whining for attention. So Royce did something about that. He dropped his left hand to her bottom, lifting her so that her sex was aligned with his.

Her moan got louder.

Her grip on his back tightened.

And the kiss got deeper and hotter.

Her taste was so familiar, like something he'd

had but still wanted. The little voice got quieter, maybe because of the roar in his head now. Also because his body was already moving onto other things.

Like touching her.

Royce slid his hand beneath the loose pajama top and eased his fingers over her right nipple. It was already tight and puckered, ready for him to do a little exploring.

And tasting.

Yeah, he apparently intended to make that particular mistake, too. He shoved up the pajama top and looked at her for a moment. Just to see if she was going to stop this.

She wasn't.

There was only the welcoming heat in her sizzling blue eyes. Not an ounce of hesitation. And it was Sophie who caught onto the back of his neck and pushed his mouth toward her breast.

The buzz became a full roar.

Sophie's moan became intense.

Everything did. The need, the pressure from the contact of their bodies. The taste of her in his mouth. Especially that. He hadn't remembered kissing her breasts before, but maybe he had, because that seemed like familiar territory, too. Of course, with the way they were grinding against each other, maybe he must want it to feel familiar.

While he tongue-kissed her breasts, Sophie didn't stay put. She pulled him closer and closer, until Royce figured there was only one place left to go. He dropped lower, kissing her stomach. Touching her. And going lower until he kissed her through the flimsy cotton panties.

She mumbled something he didn't catch, and almost frantically, Sophie grabbed on to his shoulders and pulled him back up to face her. She kissed him again. Also frantic, and she slid her hand between them and over the front of his zipper.

Royce saw stars and damn near lost his breath.

Because Sophie didn't just touch him, she started to lower his zipper.

That little voice in his head returned with a big, loud vengeance. He could *not* have sex with her. Not like this when she was so vulnerable. It would be taking advantage of her, and he wouldn't forgive himself for that.

That thought vanished for a second when she managed to get his zipper down and put her hand in his boxers.

Oh, man.

He was already rock hard, and that only made it worse. Her touch was like lightning and speared through him until every nerve in his body was zinging.

It took every ounce of his willpower to push

her hand away, and he had a fleeting thought that maybe it'd been this way that night in the motel. Maybe she'd touched him. Just like this. And maybe he'd touched her, too.

And maybe he hadn't resisted her.

Considering how they made each other feel, he was beginning to see just how probable that could be.

Royce knew if he didn't do something fast, then this would go well beyond the touching and kissing stage. They'd land in bed. Or on the floor or kitchen table. The sex would be hot, incredible and mindless.

But not without consequences.

And that's what he forced himself to remember.

Still, this had to go somewhere because Sophie was trying to get her hands back into his pants. If that happened, there wasn't enough resolve in the state to make him stop.

Royce turned the tables on her, and he took her wrists, gathering them in his left grip so he could put his right hand in her panties. She was hot, wet and ready, too, and that hardened him to the point of being painful.

"Don't think," she mumbled.

Bad advice. *Real* bad. It was that wet heat talking, and it wasn't making any more sense than his own heat and need.

Sophie made a sound so perfect, so feminine that it made his erection beg. Royce ignored it, again, and stroked her with his fingers. It was a special kind of torture for him, but Sophie's reaction was worth any price. Her eyelids fluttered down, half closed. Her mouth slightly opened.

She said his name. "Royce," she purred.

And she opened herself to him. She tore away from the grip he had on her wrists and latched on to the counter behind her, pushing her hips forward so that his fingers could go deeper, harder and faster.

It didn't take much so Royce didn't have to keep up the sweet torture for long. She came in a flash, her body pulsing around his fingers. That didn't help his erection, either, but Royce forced himself not to put his sex any closer to hers. He just put his arms around her and held her while her breath gutted and her body trembled.

Her eyes opened slowly, and he could still see the heat there. Well, for a few second, anyway.

And then the shock came, draining the color from her cheeks.

Her breath stalled, and the heat was quickly replaced with the stark realization of what they'd just done.

"No harm, no foul," he managed to say. It was stupid. Yeah, there'd been no harm all right, but plenty of foul. He'd had no right to touch Sophie that way.

"Oh, mercy," she mumbled, and she kept repeating it.

Fixing her clothes, she moved away from him and hurried to the sink to splash some water on her face. Her cheeks were flushed, and the glance she spared him was short and filled with regret.

"It would have been worse if we'd had sex," Royce assured her. His erection didn't buy that, but that brainless part of him had no say in this.

She glanced at the front of his jeans. Winced a little. "I'm sorry. I guess it won't do any good to tell you again I don't do this sort of thing." She waved off any response he might have had to that. "But twice we've been together now, and twice we've ended up, well, here." Sophie tipped her head to his zipper area.

He had to do something to break this tension—she looked ready to burst into tears. "You think this qualifies as our first date?"

She stared at him. Blinked. And then gave a dry laugh. "You don't want to date me." Any trace of the laugh faded just as quickly as it had come.

He shrugged. *Dating* probably wasn't the right word, but every inch of him wanted to haul her off to bed.

She went to the fridge, far enough away from

him that it should have helped. It didn't. Because he couldn't seem to take his eyes off her.

Sophie, on the other hand, was looking at everything but him. She reached to open the fridge, but her hand froze for a moment before it dropped to her stomach.

"What's wrong?" Royce hurried to her, and when he saw the stark look on her face, that took care of any remnants of what was going on behind his zipper.

She shook her head and slapped her hand onto the fridge. "I'm just dizzy. And a little queasy."

As soon as she said that, her eyes widened, and her mouth didn't drop open, but it was close.

"Maybe you need to eat something?" he suggested.

But judging from her reaction, that was the last thing she wanted. Another head shake. "What's today's date?"

Hell.

Royce didn't want to jump to conclusions. There were plenty of reasons for a person to get dizzy and feel queasy. But it was the look of near shock on her face that had him wondering if these symptoms were caused by something else.

"It's the fourth," he managed to say. And he waited, afraid to ask what he knew was on both their minds. It had been five weeks since the party at the Outlaw.

"You said we didn't have sex," he reminded her. She leaned against the fridge and looked up at him. "I said I didn't remember having sex with you. But—" Sophie groaned and turned away from him.

Royce wasn't feeling dizzy or queasy, but he was feeling things he didn't want to feel—like some major concern. "But what?"

The same emotions were in Sophie's eyes when she finally looked at him again. "When I woke up in the motel room, I was naked. We both were."

He thought about that a moment. "You were partly dressed when I saw you." Definitely. He would have remembered a stark-naked Sophie.

"I put on my underwear and was putting on the rest of my clothes when you woke up."

Oh, man. He did not like the direction this was going in. "Uh, did you feel any different?" *Stupid question.* Royce tried again. "Were there any signs on your body that we'd had sex?"

She didn't answer. For a long time. "Yes." Sophie squeezed her eyes shut, and she groaned even louder than Royce. "I didn't remember that, not until just now, but I was a little tender. And please don't make me explain that."

He wouldn't. In fact, he didn't want to be having this discussion at all, but it was necessary. "Any signs that you might be, uh, pregnant?

Other than the stuff you're feeling right now, that is."

She dropped the back of her head against the fridge and scrubbed her hands over her face. "A missed period. Things have been so crazy that I didn't notice I was late."

Royce couldn't dispute that, but a feeling that he thought might be panic started to crawl through him. Still, he tried not to show Sophie just how bad that panic was.

She pulled in her breath, looked at him again. "I never slept with Travis. Never. And whether you believe me or not, I don't have one-night stands. In fact, I haven't been with a man in over a year."

Sophie winced as if she hadn't intended to reveal that, and she pushed herself from the fridge and would have stormed off, but Royce got hold of her arm.

"Why wouldn't I believe you?" he asked.

"Because I lied about being pregnant." Tears sprang to her eyes. "And now it might not be a lie at all."

She shook off his grip and practically ran out of the kitchen. Royce went after her and caught up with her just as she ducked into the guest room. She would have shut the door in his face if he hadn't caught onto it. He didn't go to her and pull her into his arms, though that's what he wanted to do. Despite everything he was feeling—and he was feeling a boatload of stuff—he wanted to reassure her that everything would be okay.

All right, maybe not okay, but he really wanted to stop those damn tears spilling down her cheeks.

"Think back to that night," he said, hoping to get her to focus. Even though it probably wasn't a good idea to focus on what was making her cry. Still, they needed to know the truth. "What's the last thing you remember before waking up at the motel?"

She sank down onto the edge of the bed and smeared away the tears with her hand. "Kissing you in your truck."

"Okay." Royce tried to pick through his own memories. Yeah, that was there. French kissing, and he had his hand up her shirt and in her bra.

"I unzipped your jeans," Sophie mumbled.

That particular memory came back at him hard and fast. Especially hard. And he had to fight off the effects of remembering how Sophie had slid her hands into his jeans. And over his erection.

"Think back," he repeated, not easily. "We were in the truck when that happened, but where was it parked? Because all I remember is, well, nothing about the location."

"Yes." And there was enough heat in her voice to let him know that she remembered some of that nonlocation stuff, too.

"We were in the side parking lot of the Lone Star Motel," Sophie explained. "I'd already gotten a room before the party because I knew I'd be drinking, and I didn't want to have to drive back out to the ranch." She paused. "Plus, Travis was there at the ranch, staying the night in the guest room next to mine. I didn't want to see him."

"And I'd left my truck in the motel parking lot because there weren't any spaces at the Outlaw Bar."

So they were filling in bits and pieces, but the biggest piece of all was still blank.

Or was it?

Sophie stood slowly. "I need to get dressed so I can go into town and buy a pregnancy test." But she paused. "No. Scratch that. I need to go somewhere other than Mustang Ridge to buy it."

Yeah. Because she'd be seen, and something like that probably wouldn't stay a secret. "Half the town thinks you're pregnant anyway," he pointed out.

"And the other half has heard that I said it was a lie." She blinked back more tears. "I just don't want to feed the gossips."

Well, it would do that, and besides it might be safer if they headed away from Mustang Ridge.

He really needed to be working on the investigation, but Royce figured his focus would seriously be lacking in that area. Best to get this pregnancy question settled once and for all, and then he could, well, figure out the next step.

A baby.

Man, he hadn't seen this one coming, and he couldn't even wrap his mind around it.

"Just wait for the test result before you get upset," Sophie mumbled. And he wasn't sure if she was talking to him or herself.

She picked up her clothes from the dresser and motioned for him to turn around. "I know. At this point, modesty seems too little, too late."

Yeah, it did, but with the heat and confusion rifling through his body, it wasn't a good idea to see Sophie strip down.

Royce turned away, but he could still hear her dress. Could feel her, too. And maybe it was that combination of sensations that triggered something in his head. He whirled back around.

Not the best idea he'd ever had.

Sophie was standing there in just her bra and panties while she reached for her jeans. She froze. "What's wrong?"

Nothing was wrong, but he realized that response was coming from the brainless part of him reacting to Sophie's nearly naked body. Her bra and panties weren't skimpy. In fact, they appeared to be cotton with no peekaboo lace, but he had memories of what was beneath that underwear.

"You have a tattoo," he said, though he didn't know how he managed to speak. His mouth was suddenly bone-dry.

She got that "deer caught in the headlights" look and nodded. When she turned, she eased down her bra strap, and he spotted the tiny flower tattoo on her shoulder blade.

"My father and brother don't even know it's there," she whispered. "It's a relic from a college trip to Scotland, and it's not in a place that many people can see."

"No," he mumbled. But he'd known it was there, just as he'd known the sounds of pleasure she made in bed.

Yeah. Those popped into his head, too.

"We need to get that test done," she insisted.

Hurrying now, she pulled on the jeans and sweater, and Sophie sat on the edge of the bed to put on the shoes she'd borrowed from Maggie. She went to the adjoining bathroom to wash her face and groaned when she looked in the mirror. Maybe because she thought she didn't look good without her usual makeup and perfectly styled hair.

She looked *good*, Royce silently argued.

Damn good.

That thought collided with the reminder of why she was rushing to leave. The test. And the possible pregnancy that might or might not be a lie. Later, Royce was sure he'd have to deal with that. One way or another. But he forced everything out of his head except making this trip. He went back to the kitchen to close down his laptop, and he grabbed his coat and keys. However, before Sophie and he could make it out the door, his house phone rang. Royce hurried to answer it, hoping it wasn't trouble.

Or his father.

He didn't want to answer questions about where Sophie and he were going.

"It's me, Tommy," the ranch hand said. "We got a problem."

The young man sounded frantic and out of breath, and Royce was a hundred percent sure that this was not going to be good news.

"I got word from one of the hands who was putting out hay in the back pasture," Tommy continued. "Two men just came over the fence. And, Royce, they're carrying guns."

Chapter Nine

Sophie waited by the front door for Royce to finish his call, but she stepped back when she saw the stark expression on his face.

"There's been a change of plans." Royce threw open the cupboard over the fridge and took out a handgun and some ammo. "There are two armed men on the property, and they're headed this way."

Her breath vanished, and Sophie couldn't even utter the *Oh, God* that started racing through her head.

Royce put the gun he'd retrieved in her hand and took out another one from the wall unit in the living room. He didn't waste any time, and Sophie was glad he caught hold of her to get her moving, because her feet seemed anchored in place.

He took her through his bedroom and into the bathroom at the back of the house, and Royce put her in the tiled shower stall.

"How close are they?" she asked, and even though her hands were trembling, Sophie got the gun ready just in case she had to fire.

"They crossed the back fence about five minutes ago." He hurried to the sole window in the room and shoved back the edge of the curtain. "That puts them about a half mile away from the house."

Not far at all. Just minutes for someone determined to get to them. And she figured these two were determined if they'd chosen to trespass on a ranch in broad daylight. Sophie could see the pasture and one of the barns, but she didn't see anyone, including ranch hands or gunmen.

"Will your hands try to shoot them?" she asked.

"Yeah." And that's all Royce said for several seconds. "Tommy's trying to get into position to stop them, but he might not have an easy shot. The two aren't making a beeline across the pasture. They're staying along the fence line where there are a lot of trees they can use for cover."

"Two of them," she repeated. "Whoever's behind this hired someone else to replace the dead gunman."

Royce made a sound of agreement and glanced at her from over his shoulder. "There might be more than two."

That caused her heart to slam against her

chest, and even though she already had a death grip on the gun, Sophie's fingers clamped harder around it.

"I can't call the deputy," Royce said. "It'd leave the sheriff's office unmanned. But the ranch hands are all armed and are good shots."

Royce's cell rang, and without taking his attention from the window, he yanked out the phone, placed it on the sill and put the call on Speaker. Probably to free up his hands in case of attack.

"Royce, I lost them," she heard the man say. Tommy, no doubt. "They went back over the fence by the west barn and disappeared into the woods."

Royce mumbled some profanity. "Come back closer to the houses. You said you've warned my father?"

"Chet knows. I told him to stay inside like you said, but I doubt he'll listen."

"He *won't* listen," Royce verified. "Just watch out for him because he'll be out there somewhere."

Royce punched the button to end the call, shoved the phone back into his pocket and grabbed her hand again. "I need to be at the west side of the house, to keep watch and back up Tommy. And I don't want to leave you in here alone. Not with the window so close to the shower."

Sophie couldn't agree fast enough. She definitely didn't want to be alone, and besides she might be able to provide some backup, too. She wasn't a marksman by any means, but she had fired a gun before on one of the visits to the ranch when she was a teenager.

Shutting the bathroom door, Royce led her back into his bedroom and positioned her on the side of the dresser before he hurried to the window. He pulled up the blinds and stood to the side so he could look out.

"Stay down," Royce warned her.

She did. Sophie could no longer see the outside, but she could see Royce, and if he spotted the men, she'd be able to tell from his body language.

The seconds crawled, but her thoughts didn't. They were racing through her head. She wanted to catch these men and demand to know if it was indeed Travis behind all of this. It was sickening to know that someone wanted to harm Royce and her.

And for what reason?

It certainly seemed an extreme reaction for a man scorned, but then Travis was often an extreme person. A dangerous one, too, she added. Maybe the scorned feelings had mixed with his need for revenge for her encounter with Royce and it had brought them to this. Now it wasn't just Royce and her. Chet and the ranch hands were in the middle of this.

Even though Sophie had braced herself for an attack, the sound still sent her heart to her knees.

A gunshot.

It was deafening. And that caused her breath to gust because the shot had been fired very close to the house.

Royce didn't get down or duck out of sight. He threw open the window and pushed out the screen. She started to yell for him to get down, but she couldn't. If the gunmen didn't already see Royce, then her voice might give away their position in the house.

There was another shot.

Then another.

Both were thick blasts that seemed to shake the entire house. They definitely didn't seem like shots fired from a handgun but rather a rifle. That could mean the gunmen were far enough away from the house to possibly be out of Royce's shooting range.

But maybe not out of the ranch hands'.

Of course, anyone out there was in danger of being killed.

Royce took aim and fired. His shot rattled the panes in the window. Rattled her, too, because the men were likely converging on the house.

Another shot came flying through the window, and glass flew across the room, some of it landing on the bed and clattering onto the floor next to her.

"Stay back," Royce repeated.

She did, but Sophie caught a glimpse of the movement in the yard. A man wearing camo and a black baseball cap ducked behind a tree, and that put him much too close to the bedroom.

Much too close to Royce, too.

Royce leaned out again, directly in front of the window, fired and ducked back behind cover.

The gunmen returned fire, the bullets pelting into the window and the side of the house. Sophie saw the spray of drywall and wood and realized some of the shots were tearing through the exterior wall and coming into the room. But they weren't just coming from the direction of the bedroom window, they were also coming from the back of the house and ripping through the bathroom, as well—where Royce and she had been just minutes earlier.

"We have to move," Royce insisted. "Get down as low as you can and crawl into the living room to the side of the sofa."

Sophie dropped to her belly and started making her way there. The shots didn't stop. In fact, they were coming at them even faster.

Her heart was in her throat now. Racing out of control. And even though her hands were shaking, she tried to keep a firm grip on the gun in case she had to help Royce return fire.

It seemed to take hours for her to get from the bedroom to the sofa, and she pressed herself against it, making room for Royce. He didn't come right away, something that didn't help her racing heart, but he finally scampered out of the bedroom and slammed the door behind him. He'd barely gotten to her when his phone buzzed.

Volleying his attention between the doors and windows, he took the call on Speaker.

"We got a problem."

Not Tommy, but it was a voice she recognized. It was Royce's father, Chet. "Just got a call from one of the hands. Tommy's been shot, and he's pinned down by the side of your truck."

Sophie's breath vanished. *Oh, God.* The man trying to protect her had been hurt. Maybe worse.

"I've already called for an ambulance," Chet said, "but you know those medics can't get to him with all this shooting going on. I'll see what I can do to get to Tommy and help him."

"No." Royce glanced at her, took her by the shoulder and pushed her flat on the floor. "Stay put," he insisted. "I need you to make sure neither of the gunmen gets into the house with So-phie."

"You gonna help Tommy?" Chet asked.

"Yeah. Just make sure you watch the house."

And with that, he ended the call.

Sophie frantically shook her head. "It's too dangerous for you to go out there."

"It's too dangerous for Tommy if I don't help," he countered. Royce didn't give her a chance to disagree. "Lock the door behind me and then get back down. If anyone you don't recognize comes through a window or door, shoot him. And don't even think about following me."

The warning had barely left his mouth when Royce raced toward the door and hurried out.

ROYCE HATED THE IDEA of leaving Sophie alone in the house, but there was no other option. It was too dangerous for his father to try to cover the distance between the main ranch house and Royce's truck. There was too much open space where Chet could easily be gunned down. Plus, the gunmen had the upper hand. They'd clearly established position where they could pick off anyone and everyone who tried to make it to the wounded ranch hand.

But maybe the gunmen wouldn't count on someone coming from the front of Royce's house.

And that's exactly what Royce planned to do.

He only hoped his father could manage to stop anyone from getting inside. Chet still had a good aim. Good eye, too. So maybe Chet could keep these would-be killers away from Sophie. And there was no doubt in his mind now that they'd come here to kill rather than kidnap. If they'd wanted her alive, they wouldn't have fired all those dozens of rounds directly into the house.

Royce paused a moment on his front porch until he heard Sophie lock the door as he'd ordered her to do. He wished he could have taken the time to reassure her, but any reassurance at this point might be a lie. Yeah, they had more ranch hands than gunmen, but the hands weren't hired assassins.

He went to the end of the porch and peered around the side of the house. Royce immediately spotted his truck that had been riddled with bullets.

And he spotted Tommy.

The ranch hand was on the ground between the house and vehicle, and Tommy had his left hand clutched to his shoulder. There were blood on both his hand and jacket.

Hell.

He had to do something fast or Tommy might bleed to death. It wouldn't take the ambulance that long to respond, but Chet was right about the medics not being able to come in with bullets flying.

Keeping low, Royce eased over the porch railing, his boots landing without sound in the snow.

Of course, being heard wasn't a huge concern since the din of nonstop shooting was deafening. The shots gave him another advantage, too. Royce was able to pinpoint the location of the shooters.

One was still behind the massive oak only twenty yards or so from his house. The other was farther toward the back and was firing into the bathroom.

Keeping close to the house, Royce inched his way toward the truck. He had to do something about the shooter behind the tree to stop any other bullets from slamming into Tommy.

But how?

How could he draw the SOB out into the open so he could stop him?

A noise distraction wouldn't work, so Royce pushed aside some snow and located a rock. Using his left hand, he hurled it in the direction of the tree and immediately took aim. The moment the rock hit, he saw the movement.

The gunman pivoted out from the tree.

And fired.

Directly at Royce.

Royce fired, too, and he dove to the side so he could use the front of the truck for cover. His shot smacked into the tree, but as soon as he could, he fired another shot. And another. He knew from the sound of that one, that it hadn't hit the tree.

The gunman dropped forward, collapsing onto the snowy ground.

One down. One to go. But Royce hoped that he could at least keep one of them alive so he could question the moron and confirm who was behind this assassination attempt.

Royce shifted his attention to the back of the house where the sounds were still coming from, and he hurried to Tommy. He'd been right about the blood loss.

Way too much.

And Royce had to rethink his plan to keep the second one alive. The sooner the gunman was eliminated, the sooner he could get that ambulance on the grounds.

"I'll get you some help," Royce promised Tommy.

Tommy nodded, and Royce moved away from the injured man to the back of the truck. When he peered around the corner of the house, he immediately spotted the gunman in the doorway of the barn. That meant he was literally dead center of Royce's house. Worse, the man would see Chet if he came from the main house, and he'd see Royce if he ducked out of cover.

They needed some kind of diversion, and with the guy's position, a rock toss wouldn't get the job done.

Royce took out his phone and called his father.

"I need you to open your front door," Royce instructed, "and start firing into the ground at the front of the barn. Don't take any chances and don't lean out too far." He didn't want anyone else shot today.

"What you thinking of doing?" Chet asked.

"I need to get from my truck to the left side of the barn and then to the back." It wasn't much of a plan, but it would end this situation the fastest.

"You planning on sneaking up behind this bastard?"

"Yeah." The barn had a back entrance, and once he had it open, Royce would have a direct shot at the gunman. "Just keep the gunman turned in your direction until I can get to the side of the barn."

"Will do."

Within seconds of ending the call, Royce heard the first shot come from his father's rifle. It slammed into the snow just a few feet in front of the gunman. As expected, the guy whirled in Chet's direction and returned fire.

Royce didn't waste any time. He bolted from the corner of his house and ran toward the barn. He saw when the gunman spotted him. The man turned. Fired.

Just as Royce dove to the side of the barn.

He quickly got to his feet and started running. He tried to clear his mind and just focus on the task at hand. But that was almost impossible to do. Royce couldn't forget that Sophie was inside his house, much too close to all this gunfire. She was no doubt terrified and worried about Tommy.

Sophie would see this as her fault, and he didn't want her doing anything stupid to try to put an end to it. He damn sure didn't want her to try to surrender because this gunman clearly wasn't looking for that. He wanted her dead.

Royce rounded the corner to the back of the barn, and, staying low, he hurried to the back entrance. The shots came, piercing through the thin wood walls of the barn.

Out front, he heard his father continue with the shooting diversion, but obviously the gunman had realized that the real danger was coming from behind because that's where he was aiming now. Royce reached for the door, but he had to drop to the ground when a bullet skimmed across his jacket sleeve.

"You coward!" Royce heard his father shout. "Show yourself and quit hiding in the barn."

Royce groaned because judging from the sound of his father's voice, Chet was no longer inside the house. He was coming toward the barn where he'd be a sitting duck.

The gunman's shots changed, but bullets continued to come at Royce. The gunman must be shooting with a weapon in each hand. That would throw off his aim, but it wouldn't take much to shoot a man like Chet in the open.

"It's me that you want!" Sophie shouted.

This time Royce didn't just groan, he cursed a blue streak. He'd told her to stay put, but she hadn't listened any better than his father. Sophie was out of the house.

And right in the middle of this hellish mess.

Because he couldn't risk either Sophie or his father being killed, Royce threw open the barn door. He came in low but ready to fire.

But that wasn't necessary.

The gunman volleyed glances between Royce and the front of the barn, and Royce saw the look in the man's eyes.

Surrender.

He dropped both guns on the ground and lifted his hands in the air. "Don't shoot," the gunman said. "Let me talk to my lawyer first, and I'll tell you everything you want to know."

Chapter Ten

"You shouldn't have come out of the house," Royce said to Sophie *again*. "I told you to stay inside."

"I'm okay," she reminded him *again*. "And so is your father. You, too. It all worked out."

Well, except for Tommy, but according to the medic who'd taken him away in the ambulance, his injuries didn't appear to be life threatening. Sophie was more than thankful for that since Tommy had been shot trying to protect her.

"It worked out because we got lucky," Royce snapped. "Same for you," he snarled to his father who was in the backseat of the SUV where he was guarding the handcuffed gunman they were driving to the sheriff's office.

Clearly, she'd upset Royce by going into the yard, but there was no way she could have stayed tucked safely inside while he took all the risks. Sophie would have reminded him of that, again, if his phone hadn't buzzed, something it had been doing nearly the entire trip from the ranch and into town.

It wasn't a pleasant drive.

The snow had started to fall again, making the roads slick, and they were literally inches from the man who'd tried to kill them.

She listened to the phone conversation to see if it was an update about Tommy, but apparently it was about the gunman's body the police would have to retrieve from the ranch. It was necessary since that shooting would involve reports and such, but she figured Royce's mind was racing too much to deal with the details.

Hers certainly was.

Chet, however, seemed to have his attention honed in on the man next to him.

"I want the name of the dirtbag who hired you," Chet demanded. It wasn't his first demand. He'd repeated it from the moment Royce had handcuffed the guy and stuffed him into the SUV.

"I have to see my lawyer first," the gunman mumbled.

That only hardened Chet's glare, and even though Sophie didn't believe in breaking the law, she almost wished Chet could smack the man around and force him to talk. Especially since his lawyer would almost certainly tell him not to say anything incriminating. Judging from Royce's stern expression, he felt the same way.

Royce brought the SUV to a stop in front of the sheriff's office, and Billy, the deputy, threw open the front door for them. With Chet on one side of the gunman and Royce on the other, they practically dragged him into the building. They made a beeline for the holding cell and dumped him inside. Royce had already called the assailant's lawyer, so now it was just a matter of waiting.

Sophie hoped that *waiting* didn't include her falling apart.

Her hands were trembling, and now that the immediate danger had passed, she was reliving every moment of the attack and was painfully aware of just how close Royce had come to dying.

But it wasn't just their own dilemma.

There was the injured ranch hand and the fact that Royce's truck and house were now riddled with bullet holes. He'd also killed one of their attackers and would mentally have to deal with taking a man's life. The only saving grace was that the rest of Royce's family hadn't been at the ranch to be caught in the middle of the gunfight.

Both Chet's and Royce's phones buzzed at the same time, so while they took their calls, Sophie busied herself by going to the small break room to make a fresh pot of coffee. They probably didn't need anything to keep them alert, since they were all already on edge, but it gave her restless hands something to do. However, busy hands didn't do anything to calm her mind.

The past two days had been a whirl of attacks and interrogations. So much for her to process and come to terms with.

Too much.

Despite the aftermath of the danger, there was something else darting through her thoughts. She glanced down at her stomach and wondered if she was pregnant. The timing certainly sucked, but then maybe there was no ideal time for news like this. Either way, she would have to deal with it.

And unfortunately so would Royce.

If she wasn't pregnant, then she'd be able to give Royce a big out. One that he no doubt wanted. He'd already made it clear with the story about his mother that he didn't want a relationship of convenience. Heck, he might not want to be involved, period. It wasn't as if there was something between them. Only a possible one-night stand that neither of them could even remember. Hardly the basis for raising a child together.

Sophie frowned at the disappointment she

felt. She certainly hadn't planned on motherhood until she'd found Mr. Right and had gotten married. She was thirty, and there was plenty of time for marriage and motherhood.

So why did it suddenly seem as if this baby was exactly what she wanted?

She pushed that puzzling thought aside, blaming it on adrenaline and the fact she had just come close to dying. She'd been using that excuse a lot lately. But there was no sense being disappointed and worrying about a situation that might not even exist.

"Jake's on the way," she heard Chet relay to Royce when he'd finished his call.

She glanced up, but instead of Chet, she saw Royce in the doorway of the break room. He had his shoulder propped against the jamb and had followed her gaze to her stomach. Sophie groaned softly. He had enough on his mind without worrying about *that*.

"A problem?" he asked.

"No." She couldn't say it quickly enough, and even if there had been something wrong, like queasiness, she wouldn't have mentioned it to him. "Any news about Tommy?"

Royce shook his head, pushed himself away from the jamb and walked closer. When he got to her, he took a paper towel from the roll on the small counter and dabbed it to her forehead. Sophie was shocked to see the blood he swiped away.

"Probably a cut from the broken window," he said, his voice as tight as his expression. He wet the paper towel and wiped it again.

"It doesn't hurt," she insisted, and since there was no mirror, she glanced at her reflection on the glass front of the microwave. Sophie couldn't see any other injuries.

"It could have been much worse than a few cuts." Royce mumbled some profanity and tossed the paper towel into the trash bin. "I should have done a better job keeping you safe."

Sophie huffed. "I brought the danger to you. Not the other way around. You did everything humanly possible to keep me alive."

Nothing about his expression changed, and he leaned against the counter and stared at her.

Before his gaze dropped back to her stomach.

Sophie was afraid this was about to turn into a what-if chat so she diffused it. She slipped her arms around Royce and pulled him to her.

He made a sound, deep within his throat. A sort of rumble that she felt in his chest. He certainly didn't move away from her, and he even brushed a kiss on her forehead. Not exactly the hot kiss they'd shared at his place, but it still seemed intimate. As if they were so comfortable with each other that a kiss was a given.

"When we get a name from the gunman," he said almost in a whisper, "I can make an arrest. Then, we can see about getting that test done."

She nodded, causing her face to brush against his mouth. Again, not a kiss, but Sophie felt it deep in her blood. That seemed to be a problem for her whenever she was around Royce. She could always feel him even when he wasn't actually touching her.

Sophie heard the bell jangle and knew someone had just entered the sheriff's office. She stepped away from Royce but not before Chet saw them standing together. That was twice he'd seen them like that. And judging from his sour expression, he didn't like it any better now than he had the day before.

"Agent Lott just arrived," Chet told them.

Royce drew in a weary breath and walked out ahead of her. Agent Lott was still by the front entrance and was removing his coat and gloves, but his attention zoomed right to Sophie.

"I warned you something like this would happen," Lott snarled.

"It could have happened no matter where I was," she argued.

Lott's eyes narrowed to slits. "Not with me,

not in my protective custody. I hope you'll do the right thing now and leave with me."

Royce walked closer, his boots thudding on the tiled floor. "You pulled Sophie into a dangerous, unauthorized investigation. If you hadn't done that, she probably wouldn't have been attacked in the first place."

Lott snapped back his shoulders. "Who told you it wasn't authorized?"

"Does it matter?" Royce didn't wait for an answer. "The only thing that matters is your rogue investigation nearly got Sophie killed."

"And Royce," she added. "One of his ranch hands was shot, too."

"You're blaming that on me?" Lott huffed. "The danger would be here with or without me because of Travis's dirty dealings. It doesn't matter how or why the investigation started, but things have come to light now, and there'll be arrests."

"Then make the arrests," Royce said.

"I can't." Lott didn't seem pleased about that, either. "I needed a specific set of papers to tie Travis to all of this, and Sophie claims she didn't find them." Lott's gaze froze on her.

"I don't know what you mean," Sophie lied. Maybe it was a guilty conscience, but Lott seemed to see right through the lie. "You're not helping yourself by hiding them. And you're not helping your father."

"What papers?" Royce asked.

Sophie tried not to react, was sure she failed, and gave Royce a look that she hoped he would understand—a silent promise to tell him the truth when Lott wasn't around.

Or at least the semitruth.

Of course, she'd already mentioned to Royce that she'd found something that wouldn't paint her father in a good light, so this wasn't a total surprise. Except that Royce had no idea how important those papers were to Lott's investigation.

The silence that settled over the room was long and uncomfortable. She prayed that Lott didn't press for those papers. Prayed, too, that Royce didn't press her for an immediate explanation.

Lott pushed his thumb against his chest. "I'm in charge of this investigation, and withholding evidence is a crime."

"A crime," Royce repeated before she could respond and tell Lott to take a hike for threatening her. "Yeah. There's been quite a few of those on your watch. So, since you're in charge, you can tell me who hired that goon in there." He hitched his thumb in the direction of the holding cell up the hall.

"Oh, I will, as soon as I know," Lott insisted. "As soon as Sophie starts cooperating. And if necessary, I'll get a court order to take Sophie into custody as a material witness."

Her stomach dropped, and she whipped toward Royce. "Can he do that?"

Royce glared at the agent. "Not without a fight, and trust me, I'll fight it."

"So will I," Chet said, stepping to her other side.

Sophie didn't know who looked more surprised by that—Royce, Lott or her. She hadn't expected Royce's father to back her up.

"I'm not going to let some pissant federal agent come in here and ride roughshod over us," Chet added.

"Like father, like son, I see," Lott grumbled.

She felt Royce's arm stiffen and knew that was a major insult, but he didn't say anything. Maybe that's because some movement outside the building caught everyone's attention. A familiar car came to a stop behind Royce's SUV, and her brother, Stanton, stepped out.

Sophie didn't care for the timing of Stanton's visit. She wasn't up to chatting with anyone, but her brother had made it clear earlier that they needed to talk, so it was no surprise that he'd come.

The surprise, however, was Agent Lott's reaction.

Lott mumbled some profanity and looked at

Sophie. "You might want to rethink that protective custody."

She shook her head. "Why, because of my brother?"

"Yeah," Lott warned. "You'd be stupid to trust him."

"What the heck does that mean?" Royce asked the agent just as Stanton stepped inside.

Lott turned so that he could volley glances at both Stanton and her, and he reached in his pocket and handed Sophie a business card. It was for an Amarillo attorney that she'd never heard of.

"Who is this?" she asked. She gave the card to Royce, but he, too, only shook his head.

"Someone you'll want to call first chance you get," Lott answered. "Because Stanton did more than just take pictures of you and Royce last month. A lot more."

"Care to explain that?" Royce insisted.

But Lott ignored him. He shot Stanton a glare, grabbed his coat and gloves and headed for the door. "I'll be back with that court order to take Sophie into custody."

Chapter Eleven

Royce didn't know what to react to first—the fact that Lott was still threatening that court order, the lawyer's business card or the bombshell the agent had dropped about Stanton.

Stanton did more than just take pictures of you and Royce last month. A lot more.

Since Lott hurried out the door and Stanton was making a beeline for Sophie and him, Royce decided he couldn't delay dealing with her brother. Later, though, he'd need to make some calls to see how to stop Lott.

But there was also the issue of those *papers*.

The ones that Lott had accused Sophie of withholding. She certainly hadn't denied it. Which meant those papers were more important than she'd led him to believe.

The papers went on the back burner, and while Stanton was still making his way inside, Royce punched in the numbers on the card Lott had given him. The female assistant for Ellen Burk hart answered. Royce identified himself and told her that he needed to speak to the lawyer about an investigation he was conducting. The assistant told him that Ms. Burkhart was in a meeting but would call him back shortly.

With that out of the way, Royce turned to Stanton, who was now standing directly in front of him. "What did Lott mean about the pictures?"

Stanton didn't have much of a reaction. It was as if he'd expected the question. Probably had. He glanced at Billy and then tipped his head to the sheriff's office. "We should discuss this in private."

Sophie groaned, but inside Royce was having a more serious reaction. *Mercy.* What the devil had Stanton done and had it nearly gotten Sophie killed?

"I'll head back to the ranch," Chet said to them when they started out of the reception area.

Royce glanced back at him, nodded and made brief eye contact to thank his father. Later, he'd make that a real thanks for Chet's part in staving off the attack. Royce led Sophie and Stanton to Jake's office just off the reception area, and he shut the door.

"Start talking," Royce ordered Stanton.

Sophie's brother didn't exactly jump into an explanation. He first helped himself to a drink of water from the cooler in the corner. "I drugged you," Stanton said, still with his back to Sophie and him.

Even though it was just three little words—not much to process at all—it took a few moments to sink in.

It didn't sink in well.

"You did what?" Royce took a step toward him.

"I drugged both of you," Stanton repeated. "I put some Rohypnol—roofies—in your drinks when you were at the Outlaw Bar."

"My God." And Sophie repeated it several times. Her voice was all breath now, and she, too, walked closer to Stanton. "Why?"

Royce didn't want to wait for the *why* because there was no reasonable explanation for this. *Mercy.* Now he knew why he couldn't remember anything.

"Have you lost your mind?" Royce charged forward, ready to beat him senseless, but Sophie reached him first and held him back. "What you did was stupid, reckless. Hell, even dangerous."

"I want to hear what he has to say," Sophie insisted. "And then you can punch him."

Good. Sophie and he were on the same page there. Of course, he hadn't figured she'd be happy about her brother drugging them. There could be no good reason for that.

Stanton wiped his forehead with the back of

his hand and leaned against the desk. "I wanted to break up Travis and you. I didn't want you to have to marry that SOB." And that was it, apparently what Stanton considered to be a reasonable explanation for what he'd done.

"So your solution was to drug me and a deputy sheriff?" Sophie's voice wasn't a shout, but it was close.

"I needed a way to get those pictures so I could show Travis. I figured if he saw them, he'd break things off with you."

"Or kill us." Sophie huffed, cursed and let go of Royce. This time, he caught her since she seemed ready to slap her brother. Stanton deserved a slap, maybe more, but Royce didn't want Sophie to have to be the one to deliver the blow.

"Why me?" Royce asked. "There were others at the party that night."

Stanton lifted his shoulder. "I saw you looking at Sophie a couple of times. I thought you were interested in her. Besides, you weren't in a relationship with anyone else, and based on those looks, I didn't think you'd mind making out with my sister?"

Sophie went back to repeating some *Oh, God*'s. "Stanton, Royce and I didn't just make out. We ended up in the motel. Did you plan that, too?"

His eyes widened, and the color drained from

his face. "No, of course not. I didn't intend for things to go that far."

Sophie's hands went on her hips. "Then explain how you meant it to go."

Stanton nodded, swallowed hard. "I took the pictures of you kissing while you two were in Royce's truck, and the plan was for me to get Sophie out of there. But when I went to my car to put away the camera, there were some deputies doing Breathalyzer tests. I flunked, and they took my keys."

Sophie looked at Royce to verify if that could have happened. He had to nod. "Jake had a couple of deputies from nearby towns come in and do the tests so we could cut back on DUIs and accidents."

Stanton made a sound of agreement. "They wouldn't let me leave, and by the time I passed the test an hour later, I couldn't find either of you."

"Because we were in the motel," Sophie informed him through clenched teeth.

Her brother squeezed his eyes shut a moment. "God, I'm so sorry. What happened? I mean, did you..."

That was one apology Royce wasn't about to accept. "I have a vague recollection of us walking over to the motel. Or rather staggering there.

But I don't remember what happened once we were inside, because you drugged us."

That hung in the air between them for several long moments. "I didn't mean for things to go this far. I just didn't want Sophie to have to marry Travis."

"Neither did I," Sophie said. "But this wasn't the way to make that happen."

Stanton paused, studied her face. "You're not still marrying Travis, are you?"

"No," she snapped. "I prefer not to say 'I do' to someone who's possibly trying to kill me."

"Then I stopped it," Stanton concluded, suddenly not sounding so apologetic after all.

"Yes, you did," Sophie agreed. "But as plans go, this one sucked. For heaven's sake, Stanton, did you even think it through? I mean, without the marriage you and Dad lose everything. How were you planning to fix that, huh?"

"I'm trying to work out a deal with some, uh, loans of sorts so I can expand the ranch and bring in more livestock."

Royce glanced at Sophie, but she clearly didn't know anything about this.

"Your father's credit is shot," Royce reminded him. "Probably yours, too. Just who's willing to lend you that kind of money?"

Stanton dodged his gaze. "I'd rather not say, not until the details have been worked out."

Sophie groaned again. "You're not going to a loan shark?" She didn't wait for him to answer. "Because that hasn't worked out well so far for the family." She stopped, stared at Stanton. "Does this deal involve anything illegal?"

The knock at the door stopped Stanton from answering, not that he would have anyway. Before Royce could tell the person knocking that they didn't want to be disturbed, the door flew open, and Eldon hurried in as if there were some kind of emergency.

"What's going on here?" Eldon asked. "What's happened?"

Royce wasn't sure he wanted to get into Stanton's drug confession, especially when there were so many other things to discuss.

"Someone tried to kill Sophie and me *again*," Royce explained to Eldon.

Eldon immediately looked past Royce and at Sophie. He went to her and pulled her into his arms. "Travis did this?"

She shook her head and eased back so she could face him. "We're not sure, but Royce does have one of the gunmen in custody, and he says he'll tell us who hired him when his lawyer shows up."

Royce was glad he was watching Eldon's expression because he didn't miss the man's blink. It was just a split-second change of expression before Eldon became the loving father again. He gave Sophie's arm a pat, and then he hugged her again.

"I need to talk to this gunman," her father insisted, turning his attention to Royce. "I need to find out if, well, if the loan shark hired him to come after Sophie."

Maybe that explained the blink, but Royce wasn't feeling very generous about taking anyone, including Eldon, off his list of suspects.

"I can't let you question him," Royce explained. "He's already made it clear that he won't talk without his lawyer, and besides, this is an official investigation. I can't let civilians go in there and question a suspect. I've already called in the Rangers to assist me with the interrogation."

Not because Royce didn't think he could do the job, he could, but he wanted a Ranger present. There was a clear conflict of interest here since Royce himself had been one of the gunman's targets and therefore couldn't be impartial. He didn't want the gunman's lawyer to use that in some way to get his client out of the charges that would be filed against him.

Eldon nodded as if that was the answer he expected. However, there was also fear in his eyes. "Ask him if he's working for Teddy Bonner, the loan shark."

"Oh, I will," Royce assured him. In fact, he

would ask that right after demanding to know if the man worked for Travis.

Eldon turned, looked at Stanton. "Why are you here?"

"I had to talk to Royce and Sophie." Stanton paused and groaned softly. "Last month, I drugged them and took some compromising pictures to show Travis."

That reaction was much more than a blink. Eldon moved fast. He shoved Stanton against the wall. "You did what?" he snarled.

Sophie got between them and maneuvered her father away. Royce made sure Eldon stayed back by latching on to him.

"Stanton didn't want me to marry Travis," Sophie explained. "And he thought this was the way to prevent it."

Eldon opened his mouth, closed it. Every muscle in his body went board stiff, and he seemed too outraged to speak.

"I couldn't let her marry Travis," Stanton added. "I had to do something."

"You had to do *this*?" Eldon cursed and turned away from his son. "The attacks hadn't even happened yet. There was no reason to do anything this extreme. Besides, I still think the attacks are tied to the loan shark, not Travis."

Royce didn't like the sound of that. "Are you

saying you think Sophie should go through with a marriage to Travis?"

It took several long moments for Eldon to answer. "No." But his tone said yes. So did his body language. "He hit her. I don't want her to be with a man like that. But I have to see this from the other side, too. If Sophie could have married him, just for a month or two, then the family wouldn't lose everything."

Royce hadn't been wrong about those body language cues. Eldon still wanted this marriage. And while he didn't agree with Stanton's drug plan, Royce was glad it had succeeded in ending Sophie's engagement.

Of course, it might have created another situation if she was indeed pregnant. Despite everything going on, Royce was beyond anxious for her to have that test done.

Stanton moved away from the wall, fixed his clothes that had gotten askew when his father grabbed him. "There's no guarantee that Travis would have given us the money. You can't trust him. He could have married Sophie, murdered her and claimed all her money as his."

"We could have forced Travis to sign a prenup," Eldon pointed out.

"Again, no guarantees," Stanton reminded him. "Besides, you and I created this financial mess. Not Sophie. She shouldn't have to pay for what we did." He looked at Royce and his sister. "I'm really sorry about what happened."

Stanton didn't wait to see if his apology would be accepted, and he turned and walked out. And Royce let him go. For now. He might still arrest Stanton for slipping Sophie and him that drug, but that was minor considering everything else that was going on.

Eldon didn't waste any time going back to Sophie and pulling her into his arms. "Your brother's right about one thing," Eldon said softly. "I shouldn't have asked you to get me out of this financial mess."

Royce saw her grimace, and he figured she was feeling a lot of things right now. Anger for what Stanton did. Fear from the attack. But she also clearly loved her father and maybe saw this as a failure on her part.

"Stanton said he's trying to work out something to have the debts paid off," Sophie told her father. "Any idea what?"

Eldon eased away from her, and like Sophie, there was a boatload of concern in his eyes. "No. But I'll find out and let you know." He kissed her cheek. "I love both Stanton and you, and I know you were just trying to help me by marrying Travis. I'm so sorry it's all come to this."

There was nothing but fatherly love in Eldon's tone and in the last look he gave Sophie before he walked out. It didn't take Sophie long to react to that fatherly love, either. She groaned, made a sound of pure frustration and rubbed her hands over her face.

"I hate to see him like this," she mumbled.

Yeah. Fatherly love could create a lot of guilt. Royce didn't have that problem because Chet wasn't loving. Well, not like Eldon, anyway. And it made Royce wonder. Eldon hadn't begged and pleaded with Sophie to go through with the marriage to Travis, but maybe he thought that fatherly love/guilt was enough to push Sophie back in Travis's direction.

"Do you trust him?" Royce came right out and asked.

Sophie opened her mouth as if she might jump to say yes, but she only shook her head. "I want to trust him. Stanton, too." She paused. "But Stanton drugged us, and my father, well, he hasn't been a saint, either."

Royce thought about that a moment. "You're not just talking about his bad financial decisions, are you?"

"No." And she paused again. "I have papers that prove my father's involvement in one of the illegal land deals with Travis."

"Papers," Royce repeated. "The ones that Lott mentioned?"

"Yes." She said it so softly that he didn't actually hear the response. Royce only saw it form on her mouth.

"I want to see them," he insisted.

She shook her head. "If you do, you'll have to arrest my father."

Hell. Definitely not good. Royce hated to put Sophie in this position. Hated to see those papers. However, before he could do just that, his phone buzzed, and when he saw the name Ellen Burkhart on the screen, he knew it was a call he needed to take because the attorney might have information that Sophie and he needed.

Or at least info that Lott felt they needed, anyway.

"Deputy McCall," the woman said when he answered the call. Royce put her on Speaker so that Sophie could hear.

"Ms. Burkhart, I got your card from Agent Keith Lott, and he seemed to think you could help me with an investigation." That was a generous interpretation of why Lott had given Sophie the attorney's card, but he wasn't even sure what questions he should ask the woman.

"Yes. Agent Lott said you might be calling." Sophie's eyebrow lifted, probably wondering why Lott would do that or open this proverbial door, but Royce didn't have the answer to that, either.

"I can't break attorney-client privilege," the woman went on, "so I'm not sure how I can help you."

Royce took a moment to figure out how to phrase what he was going to say. "I need info about Sophie Conway. What can you tell me about her?"

"Not much," she immediately answered. "The information I have probably isn't connected to your investigation."

"Anything you can tell us will be helpful." Royce hoped.

The woman cleared her throat. "Well, I won't give you the name of my client. You'll have to hear that from him. But soon it'll be part of court documents and Ms. Conway will find out anyway."

Sophie's eyes widened. "Not the papers about the land deal," she mouthed.

Yeah, Sophie definitely wouldn't want those in the court system since she'd said they could lead to her father's arrest.

"What will be part of court documents?" Royce came out and asked.

"My client is challenging the terms of Diane Conway's will." She paused a heartbeat. "And that's all I can tell you, Deputy McCall."

The attorney ended the call, and Royce and Sophie stood there, staring at each other. She didn't exactly seem shocked by the news.

Sophie shook her head. "I tried to challenge it, but I failed. I wanted to share the estate with my father and brother."

"So, you think Eldon or Stanton are challenging it again?" he asked.

"Yes." She wearily scrubbed her hand over her face. "Probably Stanton. That must have been what he meant when he said he was looking at other ways to get the money."

Yeah. But it did make Royce wonder why Stanton hadn't just admitted that.

He looked at Sophie and saw her blink back the tears. Royce immediately went to her and pulled her into his arms.

"My brother's desperate," she whispered. "And if I'm dead, then he and my father will inherit. Stanton wouldn't do that for himself, but he might be willing to do that for our father."

Royce couldn't argue with that. Nor could he dismiss the fact that Eldon might have something up his sleeve, too. Maybe Eldon didn't have outright plans to kill Sophie, but he could have used the kidnapping to fake her death or something. Of course, any of those bullets could have killed Sophie so it was possible the plan—if it existed—had failed.

Sophie looked up at him, and the fatigue was all over her face. It didn't take away from her good looks. Nothing could do that. But it was a reminder for Royce to put something else on his to-do list.

"When the gunman's lawyer arrives," he said, kissing the small nick on her forehead, "I'll question the guy so we can turn him over to the Rangers, and then I'll get you out of here."

Sophie didn't fight him on that, probably because she was as eager to leave as he was. Soon, though, he'd have to bring up the papers again. But not now. For now, Royce just held her close and wondered why the heck this should feel so natural.

And right.

Even though there were at least a dozen things wrong with this.

"You must hate me," she mumbled. "Your life is a mess, thanks to me."

Royce frowned and pulled back just enough to make eye contact. "I don't hug people I hate."

"Well, you should hate me." She tried to pull away from him, but Royce held on.

"It'd be easier if I did," he confessed. He groaned. Cursed. "Let's just get past some of these obstacles, and then we can, well, talk."

"Talk?" She stared at him and slid her hand over his chest.

He felt that hand slide not just on his chest. But lower. It didn't help that her breath was meeting his, and that he could practically taste her. To cool himself down a little, he did slip his hands over her body, too.

Over her stomach.

It was meant to be a reminder of some very important details they had to learn and maybe even work out. But the only reminder Royce got was that he wanted to touch her, and this time he wanted to remember every last detail of it.

And that would be a mistake.

He repeated that to himself several times and forced himself away from her. Sophie backed up, too. She stuffed her hands in the back pockets of her jeans as if to make sure she didn't intend to touch him, but the look on her face said the opposite.

Royce was certain his face was saying the same.

The staring match continued until he heard the bell over the front door jangle again. *Good.* Maybe it was the gunman's lawyer or the Rangers. Either way, it would get this situation out of the waiting stage.

"Royce?" Billy called out. "You better get out here right now."

That got Royce moving fast, and he automatically drew his gun and pushed Sophie behind him. He braced himself for another attack. For more gunmen.

But it was Travis.

The man was in the doorway, his left hand covered with blood and pressed against his head.

"Someone just tried to kill me," Travis said. And he collapsed into a heap on the floor.

Chapter Twelve

"Call an ambulance," Sophie heard Royce say to Billy.

That sent her heart racing, and she hurried to Royce's side so she could see what was going on.

Oh, mercy.

The last thing she'd expected was for Travis to be on the floor of the sheriff's office, but there he was, and judging from the blood on his hand and clothes, he'd been injured.

She and Royce went to Travis, and Sophie knelt down and put her fingers to his neck. His pulse was strong so she eased back his hand and spotted the gash on his forehead.

"Someone ran me off the road," Travis grumbled. His eyelids twitched and finally opened.

"The ambulance is on the way," Royce told him. He grabbed a handful of tissues from one of the desks, stooped and pressed them to Travis's head. "Who did this to you?"

Sophie didn't miss the skeptical edge in Royce's

voice. Yes, there was concern, too, but he probably had the same thoughts as Sophie—was this injury for real or some kind of act?

The blood was real, that's for sure, but when Royce wiped it away, she saw that the cut wasn't very big at all, and there didn't appear to be any other trauma. Still, she was glad there was an ambulance on the way.

Royce stood, and with his gun still in his right hand, he went to the window and looked out.

"How did you get here?" he asked Travis.

"Walked. My car's in a ditch on Pearson Road, about a quarter of a mile outside of town."

It was a long way to walk with a real head injury, which only increased her suspicions.

"And you're sure this wasn't an accident and that someone purposely ran you off the road?" Royce pressed.

"Yes," Travis snapped. Cursing, he sat up and pushed Sophie's hands away so he could hold the wad of tissues to his head. "It was a big-rig truck. It hit my car from behind and didn't stop until it pushed me into the ditch."

Royce glanced down at him. "Then, there'll be tire marks on the asphalt from where you tried to brake." His skepticism went up a significant notch.

With reason.

Travis could be doing this to throw suspicion

off himself. Of course, hurting himself was an extreme measure, but so were the things they'd suspected Travis of doing. He might be desperate to avoid an arrest.

"I heard you have one of the gunmen locked up here," Travis said. He wobbled, or else pretended to, and he eventually got to his feet.

"Yeah," Royce confirmed. "He says he's willing to give up the name of the person who hired him. Does that make you nervous? Is that why you're really here?"

Travis's eyes narrowed. "I'm *really* here because someone tried to kill me, and you're a deputy sheriff. I want an investigation, and I want that SOB driver of the truck caught and thrown into jail."

Outside, she heard the wail of the ambulance siren, and it pulled to a stop in front of the building.

"Once the doctor checks you out," Royce said, "come back and fill out a report. I'll get out to the crash site first chance I get."

"Do that," Travis snarled.

The door flew open, and two medics rushed in, but they weren't alone. A tall sixtysomething man wearing a suit stepped in behind them.

"Alfred Davis," the man announced. "I'm here to see my client, Jimmy Haggard. I understand you have him in custody."

Good. That meant they might finally have some answers. Well, from the gunman, anyway. They might not know the truth about Travis until the doctors examine him. And even then they might not know if he'd managed to fake this.

The two medics led Travis to the ambulance, but Travis kept his attention on Sophie. "I'm not the one who wants you dead," he told her.

He waited as if he expected her to say she believed him. She didn't. And after several moments, Travis added more profanity and walked out with the medics.

"Call me when you know his condition," Royce said to one of the medics just as the phone on Billy's desk rang. "And get me an update on Tommy Reeter. He's in surgery to remove a bullet that this guy's *client* put in his shoulder."

"Busy day," the lawyer mumbled, and he kept his eyes on Travis until the man was in the ambulance.

Sophie followed the lawyer's gaze. "You know Travis Bullock?" she asked.

"No. Why should I?" Davis looked past her and at Royce. "I need to see my *client*," the lawyer crisply reminded him in the same tone Royce had used earlier.

Royce headed toward the holding cell, but Billy called out to him. "That was your brother on the line. Jake said he's on his way here."

Royce groaned. Jake had too much on his mind right now to be dealing with this, but Sophie welcomed the help.

"You can't go into the interview room," Royce said to her. He unlocked the cell and moved the handcuffed gunman into the interrogation room. "But there's a two-way mirror, and you can watch from Jake's office."

Once Royce had Haggard and his lawyer in the interrogation room, he stepped inside Jake's office with her. He pulled out the chair and had her sit.

"I'll see about getting you something to eat. You look ready to fall flat on your face," Royce remarked.

She felt it, too, but Sophie kept that to herself. Besides, Royce had had just as tough a day as she had, and he still had an interview to conduct.

"We'll get to the bottom of this, I swear." And he brushed a kiss on her cheek. However, he didn't leave. While he called the diner and asked for sandwiches to be delivered, Royce watched the lawyer and gunman as they whispered to each other.

"Whispering's not a good sign," she said to Royce when he finished his call. "Davis is no doubt advising his client to stay quiet."

"They're cooking up something," Royce agreed. "You think Davis recognized Travis?"

"Maybe. He was certainly giving Travis the once-over." Perhaps because Travis had been the one to hire his client, but what they needed was proof of that.

"I'll tell Davis that the interview will start as soon as the Rangers arrive," Royce said.

He gave her another quick kiss, this one on the mouth, before he clicked on the intercom mounted on the wall and strolled out as if nothing out of the ordinary had just happened. There was nothing ordinary about his kisses.

Nothing ordinary about the man, either.

Sophie sat there, the feel of his kisses still going through her, and she groaned. She was in real trouble here, and it wasn't just from the danger. She was falling for him. Hard.

She watched as Royce went back into the interrogation room, but he'd hardly made it through the door before the lawyer stood. *Uh-oh.* Sophie figured the man was about to put a quick end to any interview.

"We want a plea deal," Davis said, surprising her. But Sophie figured without a deal, the gunman wouldn't volunteer anything, putting them right back to square one.

Royce's hands went on his hips. "Your client took shots at several people, including me. I'm not exactly in a charitable mood."

"He wasn't there to kill anyone," Davis argued.

"Coulda fooled me. My ranch hand, too. He's the one who got shot."

"An accident, I assure you. My client was hired to find Sophie Conway and talk to her, that's all."

Sophie jumped to her feet. The comment was so ludicrous that it was insulting. There'd been no attempt to talk, only the attack with a hail of bullets.

"Talk?" Royce repeated. She heard the raw anger in his voice. Saw it even more in his body language.

Haggard, who was seated at the table, calmly nodded as if he didn't have a care in the world. "I got written instructions to talk to the woman and give her a phone number. The man who hired me wanted to speak to her."

Royce walked forward, practically pushing the lawyer aside so he could get in the gunman's face.

"What number and who gave it to you?" Royce asked, slapping his fists onto the metal table and getting right in Haggard's face.

"You didn't agree to the plea deal."

That didn't help ease the tension in Royce's expression. "I'll tell the D.A. you cooperated and see what can be worked out. And that's the best offer I can give you."

Haggard hesitated, then shrugged. "The whole deal was brokered through a third party. And before you ask, you can't speak to him because you shot and killed him."

No, no, no! That was not what she wanted to hear.

Sophie moved closer to the window, until she was so close to it that her breath fogged the glass. She wanted to get a good look at Haggard's face so she could see any signs that he might be lying. But the man was no doubt a good poker player, because he wasn't revealing anything.

"When you surrendered back at the ranch, you said you'd tell me the name of the person who hired you," Royce reminded Haggard.

Another shrug. "The man's name is Lucky Monroe, and like I said, he's dead."

Royce groaned, stepped back, but his hands stayed balled up into fists. "So, this Lucky Monroe hired you?"

Haggard nodded, and his carefree expression turned smug. "I guess you're sorry now that you killed him, huh?"

Royce's gaze sliced back to the man. "No. The only thing I'm sorry about is that I didn't take you out, too."

"Deputy," the lawyer warned.

"Your client is scum," Royce informed him

right back without taking his glare off Haggard. "Where's this so-called phone number you were supposed to give Ms. Conway?"

Haggard lifted his hands, the cuffs clanging against the table, and he spread his fingers to reveal the writing on his left index finger.

Royce took out his phone and pressed in the numbers. Sophie waited, her lungs aching because she was holding her breath. She prayed it wasn't her brother or father who would answer that call.

The seconds crawled by, and she finally heard Royce curse. He jabbed a button on the phone and shoved it back in his pocket. "I got a recording. The number is no longer in service."

Both relief and disappointment flooded through her. This would have been so much easier if Travis had been on the other end of that line. Of course, it didn't make any of their suspects innocent. It only meant the person after them had covered his tracks.

"Since Lucky Monroe couldn't have disconnected that number," Royce said, "any idea who did?"

Haggard shrugged again but didn't say a word. Sophie tore her attention from the man when she heard the front door open, and she went to the doorway to make sure it wasn't another visitor they didn't want.

However, it was Jake.

Royce's brother glanced down at the blood drops on the floor. "From Travis Bullock?" he asked Billy, and the deputy verified that it was.

Jake stepped around them and made a beeline toward her. "Are you okay?" he asked.

"We're alive," she settled for saying and tipped her head to the interrogation room. "Royce is in there with the gunman and his lawyer, but they're not saying much."

"Figures," Jake grumbled. "I'll see what I can do about getting Royce and you out of here."

Sophie shook her head. "But what about your daughter?"

"She's fine. Maggie and my sister are with her, and none of us will be going back to the ranch until we're sure the danger has passed."

Which might not be for weeks.

It sickened her to think of that. Jake's little girl should be home, recovering from her ordeal, but there was no way that could happen with the gunman's boss still calling the shots.

"I'm sorry," she said to Jake.

He nodded. "Not your fault."

Jake walked away and into the interview room. She couldn't tell from Royce's face if he was glad to see his brother or not.

The two brothers stepped out into the hall, and

even though Sophie couldn't hear what they said, the end result was that Jake went back into the interview room and Royce came to her. Sophie expected him to say they were leaving, but he stood in front of her, not moving.

"I need those papers," he said.

Her breath stalled a moment. She certainly hadn't forgotten about the papers that would incriminate Travis. And her father. But with everything else going on, she'd pushed them to the back of her mind.

Royce obviously hadn't done the same.

With reason. Those papers could perhaps put Travis behind bars and stop the attacks, and even though it could cause her father's arrest, too, she couldn't put that above the safety of Royce and his family.

Sophie nodded. "They're in a safety-deposit box in Corner's Lake." It wasn't far, less than ten miles from Mustang Ridge, but she stepped into the hall so she could glance out the front window. "How bad do you think the roads will be?"

"We can get there," he assured her. Royce blew out a long breath. "I'm sorry you have to do this. Sorry that I couldn't find another way."

Yes, so was she.

They started toward the front, with Royce

grabbing their coats that he'd dropped onto his desk, but before they could even put them on, Royce's phone buzzed. He took it out, glanced at the screen.

"It's Special Agent Kade Ryland," he let her know. "My friend at the FBI." As Royce had done before, he put the call on Speaker.

"Royce," the agent said. "This is a heads-up. Lott managed to get a court order to put Sophie Conway into protective custody."

Her breath didn't just stall, it stopped for several seconds.

"How the hell did Lott get that?" Royce asked. His voice was tight, the emotion barely under control.

"I'm not sure," Ryland answered. "He pulled some strings, that's for sure. Oh, and get this. The investigation is all aboveboard now. Well, as aboveboard as the paperwork says it is."

Oh, mercy. Normally, a legal investigation wouldn't have caused her heart to race out of control, but she didn't trust Lott. And besides, he was a suspect in these attempts on their lives.

"Any way you can stop the court order?" Royce asked. She hadn't thought it possible, but his jaw muscles tightened even more.

"Sorry, no. It's too late for that," Agent Ryland

answered. "Lott's on his way to the sheriff's office now to take Sophie into his custody. I figure you've got ten minutes at most to get her the heck out of there."

Chapter Thirteen

This was not how Royce wanted things to play out.

He didn't want to be on the run with Sophie, especially with the snow coming down, an FBI agent on their tails and no answers to help them stop another attack.

Still, they had no choice. He couldn't let Lott take her into custody, because Royce wasn't sure he could trust the man. Of course, there were several people on his do-not-trust list, including Sophie's own father and brother.

Royce checked his watch again. Only a few minutes since the last time he'd looked, but time seemed to have stopped while Sophie was inside the secure area of the Corner's Lake Bank where the safety-deposit boxes were kept. He hadn't gone into the room with her because he'd wanted to keep watch. It was the least he could do since he was already having second and third thoughts about taking her there. But he couldn't get past his gut feeling that those papers were critical to their staying alive.

Still waiting, he stayed near the window so he could see the traffic trickling down Main Street. He'd parked in the back, just in case Lott took this route to get to Mustang Ridge, and Royce had made sure they hadn't been followed. Still, he wouldn't rest easy until he had Sophie out of there and safely tucked away somewhere.

If somewhere safe was even possible.

They'd been lucky that the bank wasn't crowded. Luckier still that it hadn't yet closed because of the weather. Maybe their luck would hold up, and the snowy roads would stop Lott or anyone else from finding them.

Royce heard the footsteps and spotted Sophie walking back toward him. She handed him the manila envelope she'd had tucked beneath her arm, and without making it too obvious that they were hurrying, they got out of there.

"Where now?" she asked as they made their way to the parking lot.

"A motel."

She slowed a little and gave him a questioning look. Maybe she was asking if that was a good idea, but Royce had no idea how to answer that. Even if a motel turned out to be perfectly safe, Sophie and he would still be alone there. And with the attraction simmering hot and fast between them, *alone* probably wasn't a good thing. Better, though, than having bullets fired at them.

They got into the SUV that he'd borrowed from Billy and drove out onto Main Street. Sophie tipped her head to the grocery store just up the block from the bank.

"We could get the test," she reminded him.

Royce certainly hadn't forgotten about the possible pregnancy, but unlike the bank, the grocery store was packed. Probably because people were stocking up on food in case the snow closed the roads.

"Too risky," he explained.

If someone recognized them, the word might get back to the person behind the attacks. Or to Lott. Either way, that wouldn't be good for Sophie and him. It was best if they kept their location as secret as possible.

Sophie didn't argue and kept her attention on the side mirror. Royce kept watch, too, and headed out of town and toward the highway that would eventually lead to the interstate. He didn't want to go too far in case Jake needed him, but he wanted to be far enough away from Mustang Ridge that he wouldn't immediately be recognized when he checked into a motel.

In the few minutes before he'd gotten Sophie out of the sheriff's office and away from Lott, Royce had managed to grab a few supplies. Definitely no pregnancy tests. But Billy had given them some sandwiches and soft drinks he'd brought for his lunch and dinner. Royce had even grabbed some cash and a change of clothes from his locker. Not that the extra jeans and shirt would fit Sophie, but she might be able to use the shirt as a pajama top.

It certainly beat the alternative of her sleeping naked.

Okay. Royce amended that.

Her sleeping naked greatly appealed to certain parts of his body, but it wasn't a good idea. Nor was thinking about her wearing only his shirt. However, he might be able to get a room with two beds. Separate rooms were out, because he didn't want her out of his sight, but separate beds might help him get through the night without going crazy.

He looked around the cab of the SUV to see if there was anything they could use while hiding out. Royce had to push away Billy's stash of cigarettes and disposable lighters, and he found something he hoped they wouldn't need.

A handgun and some extra ammo.

It wasn't much, but with everything going on, Royce would take every little bit of help he could get.

He heard the unfamiliar buzzing sound and realized it was the prepaid cell he'd taken from the sheriff's office. Jake and he used the phones sometimes to issue to temporary-hire deputies, but Royce had snagged one so he could leave his own phone behind. With Lott's FBI resources, he'd easily be able to trace Royce's phone, but he couldn't do that with a prepaid cell.

Royce shut the glove compartment and answered the call, but he didn't say anything in case it wasn't Jake or Billy. However, it was Billy, so Royce put the call on Speaker.

"Lott finally left a few minutes ago," Billy explained. "And yeah, he was madder than a hornet when he found out Sophie wasn't here and that we couldn't tell him where she was. He's threatening to bring charges against us for obstruction of justice."

Royce groaned. He didn't need this. Neither did Jake or Billy, but there wasn't a good alternative for keeping her safe.

Sophie cleared her throat, causing Royce to glance at her. "I don't want anyone getting in trouble because of me," she said. "I can call Lott, talk to him."

He shook his head. "Not a good idea. I don't want any communication with him because we might inadvertently give him clues to our location."

Plus, he didn't want to put Sophie through

Lott's intimidation tactics, especially since she might be giving in to them.

She squeezed her eyes shut a moment. "But maybe I should go with him."

"Hell, no." And Royce didn't have to think about that. "Not until we're sure we can trust Lott."

Maybe not even then.

"Jake's still tied up, questioning that gunman," Billy added. "But he said he'd handle Lott if he comes back."

Royce didn't doubt his brother's abilities. Jake was a good lawman, but he also didn't want Jake to get in trouble over this. The problem was that Royce wasn't sure how to prevent that and keep Sophie safe. What he needed was to figure out who was responsible for the attacks, stop them, and then there'd be no reason for Lott to place Sophie in federal protective custody.

"Thought you'd also want to know," Billy continued, "that the doc checked out Travis and said it wasn't much of an injury. All he needed was a couple of stitches."

"Was it self-inflicted?" Sophie asked just as Royce turned onto the interstate. He wanted to know the same thing.

"Possibly. The doc couldn't say for sure, and Travis walked out of the hospital when the doc hinted that's what might have happened."

So Travis was out and about somewhere. But so were their other suspects.

"What about the site where Travis said he was run off the road?" Royce asked Billy.

"The road's covered with ice and snow. Can't tell much until this storm passes through. Oh, and Agent Kade Ryland from the FBI called, too," Billy added. "Should I give him your number?"

Royce considered it, and while he trusted Ryland, he didn't know if there'd be some way that Travis could get the information. "Better not risk it. What did Ryland want?"

"He found out who's trying to contest Sophie's mother's will," Billy answered.

"Who?" Royce and she asked in unison. But he didn't miss the fact that Sophie held her breath, obviously bracing herself to hear the answer that would implicate her father or her brother.

"It's Travis," Billy said.

Now *that* was an answer that Royce hadn't anticipated. Apparently, neither had Sophie because she moved closer to the phone.

"How could Travis challenge the will?" she asked. "My mother didn't even mention him in it."

"It's a long legal explanation, one I didn't fully understand, but it seems as if Travis believes he has a claim to the Conway ranch because Eldon owes him a boatload of money. Travis's lawyers are saying Diane Conway *arranged* her assets so they couldn't be used to pay off debts incurred before her death."

Royce thought about that a moment and looked at Sophie. "Is it true? Did your father get some money from Travis before your mother died?"

She stayed silent a moment, too. "Maybe. You think Travis has a claim?"

"Who knows," Billy answered. "The guy could be just grabbing at straws."

Yeah. But if there was some basis to it, then perhaps Travis could get his money and back off from Sophie. Maybe that would end the threats.

Unless Travis was hell-bent on getting revenge for their possible one-night stand after Stanton drugged them.

Of course, if Travis got his hands on that money, Sophie and her family would probably be broke, but at least they'd all be alive.

If Stanton, Eldon or both were innocent, that is.

"Call me if anything else comes up," Royce instructed Billy.

He ended the call, hoping that would be the last of the bad news, and he took the ramp to exit the interstate. There were three buildings on the access road—a hotel, restaurant and a motel. He chose the latter since it would mean Sophie and he wouldn't have to go traipsing through a lobby to get to a room.

"There are a lot of cars in the parking lot," Sophie pointed out.

Royce knew the concerns; she didn't have to voice them. More cars meant more people who could possibly see them. But it also might mean the place was already full. At least he could see the registration desk through the large front windows, which meant Sophie wouldn't have to go in, yet wouldn't be out of his sight.

"Get down on the seat," Royce instructed, "and lock the doors." He got out, waited until she'd done that before he hurried inside.

"You're in luck," the clerk immediately said. "One room left."

Finally, something had gone their way. Royce used his cash to pay for a deposit and the room, and he gave the clerk a fake name. Maybe that would stop Lott from pinpointing their location.

Once he had the key to the second-floor room, Royce parked in the back, gathered their things and got Sophie into the room as fast as possible. Royce did a quick check of the room, though there wasn't much to check. Just the bedroom and a small bath. No one was inside, lurking, ready to attack, so he double locked the door and even put on the chain.

"You should eat," he said, depositing the bag of supplies on the small table.

Since the table was directly in front of a window, he closed the blinds and took a sandwich and a bottle of water to Sophie who sank down onto the foot of the bed.

"Thanks," she mumbled, and took the items from him.

But it was obvious her attention wasn't on eating. She glanced first at the envelope of papers that he'd put next to the bag. Then she looked back at the sole queen-size bed before her attention returned to him.

"There were no rooms with two beds," Royce volunteered.

Sophie shrugged. "It probably wouldn't have mattered anyway."

He knew exactly what she meant. They'd been alone two other times before—in the Mustang Ridge motel and in the kitchen at his house, and both times they'd made out.

Maybe more.

Even if nothing had happened at the motel a month earlier, plenty had happened in his kitchen.

"So we, um...wait?" she asked.

That sounded a little sexual to him, probably because his mind kept drifting in that direction whenever he was around Sophie.

Royce nodded. "Jake might get something from the gunman." He motioned toward the papers. "There might be something in those, too." Anything that would give him the name of the person responsible so he could make an arrest.

Then they could deal with the pregnancy test. Royce hadn't realized he'd been staring at her stomach until Sophie cleared her throat. She'd obviously noticed what had gotten his attention.

"No symptoms," she reminded him. "And the odds are slim since it was just that one time."

True. And Royce didn't want to speculate on how he would feel if that test came back positive or negative. Besides, it just didn't seem real that a drugged or drunken encounter could have resulted in a baby.

She stood, placing the sandwich and water on the dresser just a few feet in front of her. "Are you going to file charges against Stanton for drugging you?"

Royce shook his head. "I haven't made up my mind about that yet. But if I get proof that he's involved in these attacks, he's going to jail."

Sophie didn't argue. She just gave a resigned nod and walked closer to him. Her arm brushed against his when she went to the table and retrieved the envelope with the papers. Even though she didn't open it or say anything, Royce knew what she was feeling.

"I'll do everything within my power to keep your father out of this," he said.

"Unless he's the one trying to kill us." Her voice was a hoarse whisper, and he couldn't just see the fatigue and worry in her eyes, he could feel it.

Even though he knew he shouldn't do it, Royce reached out, put his arm around Sophie and pulled her to him. There was nothing he could say to make things better. Nothing he could do, either. So he just stood there and held her. It might have stayed a simple hug if Sophie hadn't slipped her arms around him, too.

And worse.

She pulled back just a little, met his gaze.

The fatigue was definitely there in all those swirls of blue in her eyes, but there was a spark of something else. Again, he knew exactly what because the spark was also there inside him.

The corner of her mouth lifted. "Does this qualify as our second date?" she asked.

Royce laughed before he could stop himself. He didn't know how Sophie had managed to find any humor in this mess, but he was glad she had.

He pushed the hair away from her cheek and brushed a kiss there. That was all he intended to do because even a chaste kiss between them had an edge to it. Touching her in any way always seemed like foreplay. But he didn't pull away after the cheek kiss.

Sophie turned a little at a time until her mouth was against his. Royce felt the groan rumble in his chest. Felt the heat start to rise. With all that heat, it was hard to believe there was a snowstorm outside.

"I think we both know what'll happen if this kiss continues," Sophie said, her breath brushing against his lips.

Yeah, he did know. For some reason it no longer seemed like such a bad idea.

Even though it was.

Their situation hadn't changed, and if he got her in that bed, he'd lose the focus that he needed to keep her safe. And alive.

"I should take a shower," she whispered.

It sounded like yet more foreplay, and Royce felt himself go rock hard. She waited, maybe to see if he intended to join her. He wanted that. Man, did he. He wanted nothing more than to do something about this constant ache that he had for her.

Sophie studied his eyes a moment before she gave a slight nod. "You're stronger than I am," she said. And with that totally inaccurate observation, she walked away and into the bathroom.

Hell.

He'd known this would be difficult, but he

hadn't braced himself nearly enough for being here alone with Sophie.

Royce stood there, debating if he should go after her. He had a dozen reasons why he shouldn't, and he forced himself to remember each and every one of them. He needed to go through those papers. He needed to keep watch.

And keeping watch wouldn't happen if he was having sex with Sophie.

Royce cursed again and wished that he had zero willpower so he could go into that shower with her. But instead, he grabbed the papers and got to work.

Chapter Fourteen

The water spraying on her was too hot, but Sophie didn't turn down the temperature in the shower. She wanted the heat and the steam. Because if that heat seeped into her, she might forget the other kind of fire that was roaring through her.

Royce's kiss was responsible for it.

But Sophie rethought that. She'd been burning for Royce for over a month now, and the recent kisses had just been a reminder of the obvious.

She pressed her forehead against the warm glass shower door so the water could massage the back of her neck. It, too, became a quick reminder of Royce's touch. So did the water sliding down her breasts, belly and well, lower. She had just fragments of memories of Royce touching her at the motel a month ago, but there had been that incident in his kitchen.

The one where they'd practically had sex on the counter.

Now *that* touching she remembered.

And still felt it.

The sliding water only helped her feel it more.

Made her ache more, too.

Sophie moaned, cursed and slapped off the shower. The heat and water caressing her definitely weren't helping. Cold probably wouldn't, either. In fact, she was afraid there was only one cure for what ailed her, and that cure was in the bedroom.

Maybe even on the bed they'd have to share.

Sophie got a clear image of that, too, and felt even more heat. She'd walked away from him earlier, but she wasn't sure she'd have much luck doing that again. Her willpower was shot, and even worse, she didn't want to get it back.

She stepped from the shower, dried off, but she stopped when the towel was on her stomach.

There.

That was a reminder she did need—that she might be pregnant. Sophie managed to keep that pressed into her mind until she spotted Royce's shirt that she'd draped over the towel rack. He'd taken it from the sheriff's office since she had no other change of clothing there.

His shirt made her think of the man who owned it. If it carried his scent, then she was a lost cause.

She brought it to her face and sniffed.

Lost cause, all right.

Even though it was clean, it had no doubt been in his locker at work with other clothing, and the scent had transferred. Just a trace. Just enough to remind her of that blasted heat.

Sophie got dressed in the shirt and yet another item of Royce's clothes—a pair of his boxers. She had no other clean underwear with her so she washed her own panties and bra and hoped they'd dry soon. Until they did, she would literally be clothed in reminders of a man she couldn't seem to forget anyway.

With her nerves zinging, she eased open the bathroom door and spotted Royce. Yes, on the bed. He'd taken off his boots and had his legs stretched out in front of him. His dark hair was rumpled, probably because he was idly scrubbing his hand through it while he had his attention plastered to the papers he was reading.

Everything about him was hot. That bedroom hair. His rugged face with the sexy stubble. That sensual mouth that made her crazy with heat. His hands.

Yes, those were plenty capable of creating heat, too.

He looked up and seemed to do a double take. That didn't help with her nerves, and she glanced down to make sure everything important was covered. It was. His shirt went to her midthigh, and the boxers covered far more than her panties would have.

Royce's gaze slid from her face, to her breasts and all the way to her legs. By the time he'd finished, Sophie felt as if he'd undressed her.

Worse, she felt as if she wanted him to undress her.

"They look better on you than on me," he commented.

There seemed to be something unspoken at the end of that. Maybe something along the lines of she'd look better with nothing at all. But perhaps the ache in her body was filling in the blanks for her. This had to stop.

Had to.

And Sophie repeated that to herself.

"Find anything?" she asked, forcing herself to speak. Her nerves kicked in for a different reason. Those were the papers that could get her father arrested.

"Maybe." His attention stayed on her for several more seconds before going back to the paper. "According to this, three people signed the land deal that was used to launder money. Your father, Travis and someone named Milton Wells. Any idea who he is?"

She shook her head and walked closer. "I didn't find out much about him. I did an internet search and learned he's the head of some company."

"Investacorp," Royce provided. He glanced at the phone on the bed next to him. "I made some calls while you were in the shower."

And judging from the way his forehead was furrowed, he hadn't been pleased with what he'd learned. "This Milton Wells is dirty, too?"

"Maybe not just dirty but bogus. The company no longer exists, and according to Agent Ryland at the FBI, it was likely an offshore dummy company set up to launder money and do other illegal things."

Oh, mercy. Nothing about that sounded good. "And yet my father got involved with them."

"He might not have known it was a dummy company or that they were involved in anything illegal. I need to talk to him and find out where he met this Milton Wells and how much he knows about him."

"I could call him," she suggested. It would get her mind off Royce and back on to things that could actually help them out of their situation.

"No. I'd like to keep you out of this. Ryland's working on it, and he's also working on getting the court order canceled for your protective custody."

"Agent Ryland can do that?" Sophie asked.

"He's trying."

And if Ryland managed it, Royce and she could go back to Mustang Ridge. Well, maybe. They could if they managed to neutralize the danger.

"So what happens with my father and those documents?" she asked.

"If Eldon knows anything that can be used to arrest this Milton Wells, then we might be able to work out a deal to keep your father out of jail."

Sophie hated to get her hopes up, but she did anyway. "Thank you. After everything that's happened, it's generous of you to do this for him. For me."

Royce tilted his head, stared at her. "Hey, I said I'd do everything to keep your father out of jail, and I will."

"I know."

Her words hung between them. Their gaze stayed locked. And something changed in the air.

Without taking his attention off her, Royce dropped the papers on the bed next to his phone, and he eased across the mattress toward her. Even though they weren't officially lovers, Sophie knew that look he was giving her. She saw the subtle changes in him. This was no longer about the papers and the promise he'd made to her.

This was about *them*.

She didn't go closer. Couldn't. Her feet seemed

anchored to the carpeted floor, but Royce had no trouble moving. He got to the edge of the bed, swung his legs off the side. However, he didn't get up. He caught her by the waist and inched her toward him.

"Just so you know," he said, "I don't usually do reckless things."

She nearly laughed. Nearly. "So, I'm reckless?"

"No." His cool green eyes were no longer cool. They were sizzling, like the rest of him. "You're the woman I apparently can't resist. Not resisting you is the reckless part."

He didn't seem happy about that. Neither was she because she couldn't seem to resist him, either. That didn't make things even. Or right. So, yeah, this was reckless. But Sophie didn't pull away when Royce leaned in and pressed his mouth to the front of her shirt.

To her right breast.

She had no trouble feeling his kiss through the fabric of the shirt. It was just as hot and arousing as if his mouth had touched her bare skin.

Royce didn't stop with just the breast kiss. His grip on her waist tightened just slightly, and he eased her forward. The next kiss he gave her was on her stomach. Then, lower. To her right hip bone.

Sophie's eyes fluttered down. She felt herself go from warm to hot. And she slid her hand around the back of his neck to bring him even closer. Not that she needed to do that. Royce was already moving in that direction anyway.

He kissed her. Still through the clothes. And he touched her, too. His hand slid lower, over the small of her back and to her bottom, and using that same gentle pressure, his fingers lit some new fires along the way.

"You can say no," he whispered. "You *should* say no."

His words and breath created an interesting sensation through the cotton boxers, and the sensation speared through her.

"I don't want to say no," she answered.

Sophie wanted to shout *Yes!*, grab on to him and put his clever mouth right in the center of all that heat. Better yet, she wanted their clothes off and then both on the bed. She wanted Royce to send her flying.

Royce pushed up the shirt so he could kiss her exactly the way she wanted. He went lower, shoving down the boxers and using his mouth to rev up the heat even more. But soon, it wasn't enough. Her body was burning for him, and Sophie wanted more.

He seemed to sense that, too, and as if they were in sync in both body and mind, his grip around her backside tightened, and he pulled her forward. Wrapped in each other's arms, they dropped back onto the mattress.

The kisses didn't stop, though he moved them back to her mouth and neck, all the while adjusting their positions until the center of her body was aligned with his erection pressing hard against his jeans.

Her breath caught in her throat. Her head went light, and it got even lighter when he pulled off her shirt. His, too, and his bare chest landed against her breasts. Another mind-blowing sensation.

Sophie had guessed that Royce pretty much had a perfect body, and she hadn't been wrong about that. Not overly muscled, but he was toned and tight. Yes, perfect.

The kisses got deeper, and he used his tongue on her nipples until Sophie was arching her back and begging for more. Royce gave her more. He stripped off her boxers and made his way down her body for some of those kisses she'd been fantasizing about.

Oh, mercy.

Perfect, indeed.

It didn't take long, just a few of those well-placed kisses before Sophie wanted this to go to the next level. She wanted Royce, naked and inside her.

She caught on to his shoulders and pulled him

up to go after his zipper. He didn't help, and for a moment she couldn't figure out why. Then she realized he was taking his wallet from his back pocket.

Royce pulled out a foil-wrapped condom.

Great. She was so hot and ready for this that she'd forgotten all about the basics of safe sex. Thankfully, Royce hadn't, and he put on the condom as soon as he'd taken off his jeans and boxers.

He looked at her, as if checking one last time to make sure she was okay with this. Sophie was more than okay, and she hooked her arm around his waist and brought him down to her. Exactly where he should be.

Royce entered her slowly, but there was nothing slow about her response. The sensations exploded through her. So hard, so fast. That Sophie lost her breath. She couldn't speak—her throat had clamped shut. Couldn't hear because of her heartbeat crashing in her ears. But she could feel.

Oh, yes.

Even though Royce started out gently, it didn't stay that way, and Sophie was thankful for it. This wasn't the time for gentle. She needed him. Needed this to be finished.

Royce did his part.

He moved deep and hard inside her, and Sophie wrapped her legs around his waist allowing him to lift her hips toward each of those thrusts. Royce had already given her a climax in his kitchen so she knew something about how he could make her feel.

But this was more.

The pleasure was blinding and soon unbearable.

Royce's gaze stayed locked on her, and he didn't waver. Not with the look in her eyes nor with the intensity. Sophie wanted to tell him this was perfect.

Too perfect, maybe.

She wanted to tell him to finish her. But that wasn't necessary, either. Royce moved his hand between them, touching her where they were already so intimately joined, and just like that, Sophie felt herself shatter.

The raw pleasure and relief roared through her, and the only thing she could do was hold on to Royce and let him finish her off.

Chapter Fifteen

Royce tried not to make a sound when he used the small coffeemaker in the motel room to brew a strong cup. Sophie was still asleep, and he wanted her to stay that way awhile longer, but he also needed the caffeine to clear the cobwebs in his head.

He sat at the desk where he'd left the papers and tried to study them again. Royce could see all the details of the sale. Could see that Eldon, Travis and this third man, Milton Wells, had clearly broken the law, but even after several whispered conversations with Agent Ryland, Royce still didn't know who Wells was.

Of course, the same could be said for the entire investigation. Despite the dozen phone calls and emails he'd exchanged, there'd been no breaks or new developments in the case overnight.

Unlike his relationship with Sophie.

Oh, yeah. There'd been a break there all right. Before he'd even landed in bed with her, Royce had known it would be a mistake. That hadn't stopped him, of course, and sadly it wouldn't stop him from making the same mistake again. He still wanted her, and having sex with her had only fueled that need. It hadn't satisfied it at all.

Now, the question was—what was he going to do about it?

"Nothing" would be the right answer. With Sophie's safety and this investigation hanging over his head, there's no way he should be thinking about extending this affair.

Or whatever it was.

But it was almost impossible to push it aside when they still didn't have the results of a pregnancy test. That was a result that could change everything.

He hadn't planned on fatherhood, but he wouldn't run from it, either. No. Just the opposite. If Sophie was carrying his child, then they would need to work out something. Shared custody. A relationship of convenience. Whatever it took to put and keep him in the child's life. No way would he be a bitter, emotionally absent father like his own.

However, this did give Royce a little insight into how Chet had felt about an unplanned pregnancy. It wasn't an easy matter.

Sophie didn't make a sound, but she jackknifed to a sitting position. Her eyes were wild, unfocused, and her gaze darted around the room until it landed on him. Even then, it seemed to take several seconds for her to recognize him and breathe a sigh of relief.

"A dream," she mumbled.

More like a nightmare. Royce had had a couple of those, too, during the night. Some about the investigation. Another about potential fatherhood.

Sophie threw back the covers, but then immediately threw them back on when she glanced down at her naked body. "Sorry."

His eyebrow went up. "I'm a guy. Trust me, seeing you like that isn't cause for an apology."

She made a soft sound of agreement and eased back the covers again. However, this time she grabbed her clothes and quickly started to dress.

"If you're hungry, they're plowing the roads now," Royce told her. "We could go to a drive-through fast-food place and get something."

"Maybe later." She paused and glanced at him from the corner of her eye. "How many second and third thoughts are you having this morning?"

Part of him admired her direct approach. Another part of him dreaded the answer. He wouldn't lie, that's for sure. "A few. But not for the reasons you're thinking."

This time Sophie made a sound of disagreement. "You're thinking you crossed a line by sleeping with someone you're protecting. A law enforcement no-no. You're probably also thinking this complicates things. Plus, there's that whole part about you believing I'm totally wrong for you."

Okay. So, maybe she did know the reasons for his second and third thoughts.

"I'm wrong for you," he corrected. Then shrugged. "That doesn't stop me from wanting you."

The corner of her mouth lifted, and she pushed her tousled hair from her face. Sexy hair, he noticed. Actually, everything about her fell into that category, including her generous curves and that welcoming smile that she no doubt hadn't meant to be so welcoming.

She stood, went closer, took the cup from him and had a huge sip of his coffee. "What do you want me to say? That I can be content living in a place like Mustang Ridge? That I'm not a city girl?"

"Nothing wrong with being those things," Royce admitted. "But if we were looking for something long-term, it might be a problem."

She stared at him. "Long-term?"

He let his gaze drift to her stomach. "Oh. That kind of long-term." She shook her head. "I don't want you to feel trapped."

Like your father.

She didn't say the words, but it was there in her tone and the look she gave him. "What? You don't think I'd be a good dad?" he asked.

"No. You would be," she quickly answered. "I'm just not sure it'd be fair to put you in that position."

"Fair?" For some reason, that riled him. "Sophie, none of this was fair. Your brother drugged us, and if he hadn't done that, we probably wouldn't have had unprotected sex."

"If that's what happened." Sophie dropped a kiss on his forehead.

Sophie had another sip of his coffee before she tipped her head to the papers.

"Anything?" she asked.

So sex, possible future sex and long-term plans were no longer the topic of discussion. Royce figured he should feel relieved, but he knew it was just delaying the inevitable. Eventually, they'd have those test results, and even if they were negative, the attraction sure wasn't going to dim.

"According to Agent Ryland at the FBI," he explained after he collected his thoughts, "Milton Wells from Investacorp doesn't exist. A dummy name for a dummy company."

She stared at the papers a moment and then huffed. "So, he could be anyone?"

"Yeah. But he'd still have to be someone your father knows since they signed the papers together. By the way, I tried to call him this morning, but the call went straight to voice mail."

That in itself wasn't suspicious. After all, it was early. But there was something about her father that bothered him.

"I talked to Billy this morning, too," Royce continued. "Neither your father nor brother has called the sheriff's office to find out where you are."

Royce was about to ask if that was out of the ordinary, but he could tell from the concern in her eyes that it was.

She shook her head. "Maybe Lott is with them, and they don't want to call because he might learn where I am."

That was possible. Lott would definitely go to her family or Travis to find out where she was. Still, if Sophie was his family member and essentially missing, he'd be out looking for her.

Blowing out a long, weary breath, she sank down onto the foot of the bed. "I have to at least consider my father and brother are suspects."

Royce settled for a nod. He was doing more than considering it because they both had strong motives.

Money, and lots of it.

If Sophie was dead and out of the way, Eldon would have the money to pay off the loan shark and revive the ranch. Stanton and he might also be nursing some ill feelings about being completely cut out of Diane Conway's will. But what didn't fit in that scenario was the fact that Stanton had drugged Sophie and him.

His phone buzzed, cutting off that thought, and Royce recognized the number when he glanced at the screen.

Special Agent Kade Ryland.

Royce had already spoken to the man twice this morning, but he was anxious to hear if the agent had found anything out about Milton Wells. Sophie was clearly anxious, too, because she moved closer to the phone, and Royce put the call on Speaker.

"Deputy McCall," Ryland greeted. "Hope you're sitting down for this, but the order to take Ms. Conway into protective custody has been pulled."

Royce could see the relief go through her. It went through him, too. "Thank you," he said to the agent.

"Don't thank me. Lott pulled the order himself."

That took away a little of Royce's relief. "Why?" he asked suspiciously.

"Lott says it's no longer necessary. He said he found proof of who's been trying to kill you and Ms. Conway, and he's on his way now to Mustang Ridge to make an arrest."

Sophie leaned on the desk and sank down onto the edge of it. "Who is Lott arresting?" Since her voice had little sound, Royce repeated the question so the agent could hear it.

Agent Ryland cleared his throat first. "Sophie's father, Eldon Conway. Lott's picking him up at the ranch and taking him to the Mustang Ridge jail."

SOPHIE TRIED TO TAMP DOWN the feeling of panic, but she was failing big-time.

Not long before Agent Ryland's call, she'd accepted that her father and brother could be suspects. Or so she thought she had. But it cut her to the core to know that Lott claimed to have proof of her father's guilt when her father had been the one person she'd tried to protect.

"We'll get to the bottom of this," Royce said to her. He'd already given her various assurances of that as they'd thrown their things into the SUV and started the drive back to Mustang Ridge.

Sophie hoped that was possible. "Even if Lott found the incriminating papers for the land deal, what kind of proof could there be that my father tried to kill us?"

Royce glanced at her, and Sophie saw the sympathy in his eyes. A stark contrast to the look he'd given her the night before. He also didn't hesitate, which meant he'd given this some thought.

"Jimmy Haggard, the gunman I questioned, could have named your father," Royce offered.

"But wouldn't Jake have told you?" she asked.

He shook his head. "The Rangers took him into custody late yesterday. Haggard could have worked out some kind of plea deal with them."

"And Haggard could have lied to save his own skin."

Royce reached across the seat, caught her hand and gave it a gentle squeeze.

It helped.

Well, it helped as much as something like that could. But what would help even more was speaking to her father and hearing him say he had nothing to do with this. So far, she'd had zero luck with that, since her father wasn't answering his phone. That wasn't so unusual, though, since he often forgot to carry his cell with him and the snowstorm might have interfered with service.

"Maybe it wasn't a deal that Haggard struck," she said, more to herself than Royce. She was thinking out loud, trying to make sense of this. "Maybe it was Travis. Or Stanton."

Royce squeezed her hand again. "You'll drive yourself crazy by guessing like this. In a half hour or so, we'll know for sure."

That was an optimistic timetable because the snowy roads would certainly slow them down.

Sophie refused to think of what would happen if they couldn't get through.

There was little traffic on the interstate, probably because the snowplows were still out, but Royce kept glancing at the side mirrors. No doubt to make sure they weren't being followed. Maybe that meant he didn't believe her father was guilty.

Royce took out his phone and pressed in some numbers. Since it was on Speaker, a few seconds later Sophie heard Billy answer.

"Any sign of Lott yet?" Royce asked the deputy.

"None, but then the roads are still pretty bad here. Might take him a while to get out to the Conway ranch and then back here to the sheriff's office." Billy paused. "You had a chance to talk to Eldon?"

"Not yet. Sophie's tried to call him a couple of times."

Yes, and she'd try again when Royce finished this call. She didn't want her father to try to run from Lott, but she didn't want the agent to spring an arrest on her father, either.

"I'll let you know the minute they arrive," Billy assured him. Royce clicked the end call button, handed the phone to her and took the turn off the interstate.

The ramp was mostly clear of the snow, but Royce had to slow down the moment he got onto the two lane road that would take them back to town. It would be slow going, and that didn't do much to steady her nerves.

Sophie tried to call her father again but got the same results. It went to voice mail. It was the same when she tried to contact Stanton. Like before, she left messages for them to call her and she gave the number of the prepaid cell phone.

"Nothing," she relayed to Royce.

She took a deep breath, trying to concentrate on keeping watch, but the dizziness hit her. Not an overwhelming sensation, but Sophie did touch her hand to her head.

"What's wrong?" Royce immediately asked.

Thankfully, the dizziness went as quickly as it came. "I'm okay," she assured him. "I'll get something to eat when we get to Mustang Ridge."

Royce gave her another concerned glance, but he didn't voice what they were both thinking. She really needed to get her hands on a pregnancy test—soon. But for now, Sophie had more immediate concerns.

She looked down at the phone that she still had in her hand and groaned when she saw they no longer had service. A dead zone. So, even if her father got her message, he might not be able to call her back right away.

Even though Royce didn't make a sound, Sophie heard the change in his breathing, and her gaze snapped to him. He was volleying glances into the side and rearview mirrors, and she looked behind them to see what had garnered his attention.

A semitruck.

It wasn't unusual for commercial trucks to be traveling here since the road led to several small towns, but it was obvious that Royce had an uneasy feeling about it.

"A problem?" she asked.

Royce shook his head. "I'm not sure."

He kept watch. So did Sophie. And she soon saw what had put the concern on Royce's face. The truck was going too fast, and the road was icy and narrow. Passing them wouldn't be safe.

Royce tapped his brakes, no doubt to make sure the driver of the semi saw them. But the driver didn't slow down. He continued to barrel at them. Closer. And closer.

"Hell," Royce growled. "Make sure your seat belt is on."

The warning barely had time to register in Sophie's mind when she felt the jolt that slung her body forward.

The truck plowed right into the back of their SUV.

Chapter Sixteen

Royce tried to brace himself for the impact, but there was no way to do that with the huge truck crashing into them. Their SUV was much smaller, and the snowy road didn't help. Royce had to fight the steering wheel just to keep the SUV from going into the ditch.

"Oh, God." Sophie grabbed on to the dash with both hands.

And Royce knew why. The semi came at them again, bashing into them and sending the SUV into a skid.

Royce turned the steering wheel into the skid and tapped the brakes. However, he'd barely gotten control when the truck slammed into them again. He saw the back bumper fly off, and the rear-lift door flew up.

The bitter cold air immediately rushed into the cab of the SUV. So did the roaring sounds of the semi. It was like some monster bearing down on them for another attack.

Because the semi was so high off the ground, Royce couldn't see the driver or if it was just one person in on this attack. He suspected there were others since this seemed to be an attempt to kill them.

So, who was behind this?

One of their suspects, no doubt, because the odds were sky-high that this was connected to their investigation.

The semi crashed into them again and ripped off the entire rear door. Even if Royce managed to keep the SUV on the road, it wouldn't be long before the semi literally tore their vehicle apart. Then Sophie and he would either be killed in the impact or else would have to face down whoever was doing this.

Royce risked glancing at her. There was no color in her cheeks, but she was no longer holding on to the dash. Sophie was rifling through the glove compartment, and she took out the extra gun and ammo that Royce had seen the day before. Maybe, just maybe, they'd live long enough to use that ammo on the SOB who was doing this.

"Grab one of the lighters, too," he told her.

She probably had no idea why he'd want that, but if this truck managed to get them off the road and they had to escape into the woods, the lighter might come in handy to build a fire.

Another hit from the semi, and Royce felt the back tires give way. Thank God there was no other traffic on the road, because the SUV shot straight out into the opposite lane, and they headed for the ditch.

"Hold on," Royce warned Sophie as she crammed the gun, ammo and lighter into her jacket pockets.

The adrenaline was pumping through him. His heart racing out of control. But Royce forced himself to do a split-second assessment of their situation. Yeah, they were going to crash. No way to stop that. But they would hit the ditch and beyond that there were some trees.

And even a small wood-frame farmhouse.

Maybe there was someone inside who would see what was going on and use a landline to call 9-1-1.

Royce was certain they'd need backup.

If they survived, that is.

The semi slammed into them again, clipping the back of the driver's side of the SUV. The impact completely dislodged the tire, and it flew through the air, bouncing off the semi. Royce did what he could to keep control of the SUV—it wasn't much—but he put a death grip on the steering wheel and tried to keep them on the road.

He failed.

The SUV plowed nose-first into the snow- and ice-filled ditch.

The airbags deployed, slapping into them and knocking the breath out of Royce. He immediately looked at Sophie to make sure she was alive. She was, thank God. Not only alive but able to move.

Royce moved, too. Fighting for air, he slapped down the bag and drew the gun from his shoulder holster.

Beside him, Sophie did the same and then threw open the door. Or rather she tried to do that. She only got it open a few inches before the bottom edge of the door jammed against the frozen ditch.

Royce looked out his side window and saw both doors of the semi fly open. That upped the urgency for Sophie and him, and he twisted his body so he could kick the passenger's door. With the critical seconds ticking off in his head, he gave it another kick. And another.

Before it finally flew open.

"Move!" he said to Sophie, though she no doubt understood the need to do exactly that.

She practically spilled out of the SUV and landed on the side of the ditch. Royce pushed her out of the way so he could get out, too, and then he grabbed her by the arm so they could start running. He didn't look back because he figured whoever had been in that semi was armed.

He was right.

A shot flew by them just as Royce shoved Sophie behind a tree.

Royce cursed for putting her in this situation again. And then he cursed the person responsible for this attack. He was sick and tired of Sophie being in danger and not even knowing the reason why.

Another shot came, tearing through a chunk of the tree trunk and showering them with splinters. Royce didn't return fire. Sophie had a handful of extra ammo, plus the backup weapon, but he didn't know how long this fight would go on. Best not to use any bullets until it became absolutely necessary.

He figured that wouldn't be long from now.

"How many?" she asked.

Since Sophie was about to peer out from the tree, Royce pulled her to the ground and looked for himself. "There are three."

All of them were wearing ski masks and camouflage clothes just like the other two gunmen who'd attacked them at his house. Now the new trio was using the wrecked SUV for cover, but only two of them were poised to fire.

The other appeared to be searching through the SUV.

For what, though?

Royce tried to keep an eye on him, but that was hard to do with the other two continuing to fire shots at them. Each bullet tore away more of the tree, and Sophie and he couldn't just sit there and wait to be gunned down. He needed to put some distance between the shooters and them and then get into a better position to return fire.

"There's no service out here," he heard Sophie say, and it took him a moment to realize that she was looking at the cell phone.

Royce hadn't even known that she had managed to hang on to it. It might come in handy if they could get out of this dead spot for service. Of course, even if they could call, help wouldn't get there for *a while*, but a while was better than nothing. Royce would take all the help he could get to keep Sophie safe.

With the shots still coming fast and furious, Royce glanced behind them at the pair of oaks. They were much wider than the cottonwood they were using for cover now, and it would give Sophie and him several extra feet of breathing room. Plus, it had the added bonus of being even closer to the house. He didn't want anyone inside being hurt from the gunfire, but a house would give them much better protection than the trees.

"Stay on your stomach," Royce instructed her, though he had to shout over the roar of the gunfire. "And crawl there." He tipped his head to the oak.

"What are you going to do?" she asked.

"Try to give you a diversion. It'll be okay," he quickly added when he saw that she was about to argue with him. "Hurry."

He left no room for doubt in his voice, and thankfully, Sophie stayed low and inched her way toward the oaks. Royce darted out from the cottonwood and fired. He didn't see where his shot landed because he immediately went back behind cover, but he heard the bullet strike metal. Probably one of the vehicles.

He checked to make sure Sophie was behind the oak. She was. Royce glanced out again. Not at the shooters but at the guy going through the SUV. And Royce cursed when he saw what the man had in his hand.

The manila envelope with the land papers.

Hell. How the devil had they known the papers were there? And why were they so important to retrieve during a gunfight?

Royce figured he wouldn't like the answer to either question, but both Travis and Eldon had some serious reasons for those papers to be destroyed. It was going to hurt Sophie bad if her father was wearing one of those ski masks. However, Royce couldn't let that play into this. Sophie came first.

And if her father was behind the attacks, then they'd have to deal with that later. For now, Royce just tried to even the odds.

Staying low, he moved to his left and took aim at the gunman positioned at the front end of the SUV. The one with the papers had already headed back to the semi. Out of range. But Royce figured his best chance to pick one of them off was the guy on the front end.

It was a risk, but everything about their situation was risky.

Royce leaned out from behind cover. And fired.

He double tapped the trigger and saw the man he'd targeted jerk back from the impact of the shots that Royce had just fired into his chest. For a moment, Royce thought the guy might be wearing Kevlar, but he wasn't. The man dropped to the ground.

One down.

That thought barely had time to register in Royce's head when he heard the sound. Felt it, too.

The pain seared into his shoulder as the bullet slammed into him.

"WATCH OUT!" SOPHIE shouted to Royce.

But she was already too late.

She'd seen the movement from the corner of

her left eye. Another gunman. Not the one who'd taken the papers from the SUV—he was inside the semi now. This one had no doubt made his way from the back of the semi and toward them. Sophie could only watch in horror as the man fired a shot.

One that hit Royce.

"Stay down!" Royce told her just as she started to race toward him.

He was right, of course. If she moved out from the cover of the oak, the gunmen would just shoot her, too, but it took every bit of her willpower to force herself to stay put and not hurry to Royce.

Sophie levered herself up a little so she could get a better look at Royce. She prayed that he'd manage to survive that shot, and she was more than relieved to see him moving around. He was staying behind the tree, thank goodness, but she didn't miss the blood on his jacket. She had no idea how badly he'd been hurt, but she had to do something to get them out of there.

She looked around and saw the gunman still at the rear of the SUV. The other one, the bastard who'd shot Royce, was no longer in sight. Maybe he'd ducked behind a tree, too, or he could have even headed back to the semi. There were some shrubs and even the ditch that he could be using to conceal himself.

So, there were three attackers still alive.

With Royce's normally good aim, that wouldn't have been such bad odds, but there was nothing normal about their situation.

The shots started to come again. Nonstop. Deafening. But they all seemed to be coming from the shooter at the rear of the SUV. Sophie didn't have Royce's shooting skills, but she fired a shot that guy's way. He ducked down behind the SUV.

It was a temporary lull, but Royce used it to crawl his way to her. Even though Royce was cursing and telling her to stay down, Sophie fired another shot at the gunman, to keep the attention on her. And that meant she had to keep her attention on them, to make sure they didn't try to come after Royce and her from a different direction. She considered calling for backup, and would, once she no longer had to fire shots to keep the men at bay.

Royce finally made it to her and pulled her back to the frozen ground.

"How bad are you hurt?" she asked, but Sophie was terrified to hear the answer.

"I'm okay."

It sounded like a lie and probably was. While Royce kept watch, Sophie pulled open his jacket and looked for herself. There was blood. Too much of it. Of course, any amount was too much when it came to Royce. She wadded up some of his shirt and put some pressure on the wound, hoping it would slow the bleeding.

"We need to get to the house," he said.

She looked back at the place. Not far. But every step would be dangerous, especially with those shots coming at them. Plus, she saw something she hadn't seen from the road.

The weathered For Sale sign.

Oh, mercy. That meant there might not be anyone inside to help them.

"I need the lighter," Royce added. "And any paper you might have in your pockets."

He used his hands to rake together some dead leaves and small sticks from the ground.

"They're too wet," she reminded him.

"We don't need a fire. Just smoke. And the wind is working in our favor. It'll carry the smoke toward the gunmen."

Yes. It might shield them from the shooters.

Might.

Sophie helped Royce scoop up as much debris as she could safely reach and then she rummaged through her pockets. She had a wadded-up tissue and a receipt from a coffee shop. Royce pulled out his wallet and added some twenty dollar bills to the stash.

She lit the tissue and held her breath.

The shots didn't stop. In fact, they seemed

to come at them even faster. The oaks were old and thick, and thankfully the bullets couldn't get through, but the gunmen could easily change positions and try to come at them from a different angle. Both Royce and she kept watch to make sure that didn't happen.

It didn't take long, just a few seconds for the bills and paper to catch fire, and Royce gently placed some of the damp leaves on top. He'd been right about the direction of the wind. It carried the smoke away from them.

"You have the gun with the backup ammo. So stay down and fire a shot to your left," Royce instructed. He added even more leaves to the now billowing smoke. "The gunman's moving."

Oh, God.

She'd taken her eyes off him for just a moment, but he had indeed moved and was trying to make his way closer toward them.

Sophie fired.

The gunman ducked back down just as a gust of wind caught the cloud of ashy-gray smoke and sent it coiling out in front of them.

She and Royce added the last of the debris they'd collected, and they waited for the smoke to thicken. Time seemed to stop. The only thing that did. Because the fear inside was going at lightning speed. Not for herself.

But for Royce.

They needed to get to safety so she could call an ambulance, maybe from a landline inside the house—if there was one.

"Now," Royce said.

And that was all the warning Sophie got before he latched on to her hand and got them moving. They stayed as low as possible but started running toward the house. Even over the sound of her own heartbeat roaring in her ears, Sophie heard the footsteps of the gunmen running straight toward them.

Chapter Seventeen

Royce knew the smoke wouldn't give Sophie and him much cover for long. That's why he hurried, pushing Sophie to go as fast as she could go. They had to make it inside the house so she'd have some protection.

And so he'd have position to take out these SOBs.

The shots returned, just as Royce had expected, though he figured the gunmen still didn't have a clear line of sight because of the smoke. They were no doubt just randomly firing and hoping to get lucky.

That might happen.

Royce didn't take Sophie onto the front porch. Everything about the place told him there was no one inside, that the farmhouse had been empty for months or longer. Part of the roof had caved in, the front steps, too.

So he headed for the barn.

It wasn't in much better shape than the house,

but at least there'd be no floor for them to fall through.

The barn door was wide-open, and heaps of snow-dusted hay were scattered everywhere. Royce pushed Sophie inside, and they managed to slam the door shut. There was no lock, and Royce knew they only had seconds before the shooters would catch up.

"Go over there," he told Sophie, and he motioned toward the side wall.

That way, she wouldn't be directly in front of the door. Royce took cover behind what was left of a stall. It wasn't much protection, but he might not need it because he checked the back door, and it was indeed closed tight with a thick board lock. Old-fashioned, but it looked rock solid. That meant if the gunmen tried to get inside, they'd have to go through the front.

And get by him to reach Sophie.

Royce looked over at her and hated what he saw. The fear in her eyes. And more. She was terrified for him. He wanted to reassure her that his injury wasn't that bad.

He hoped.

Yeah, he was bleeding. The warm blood was trickling down his chest from his left shoulder. There was pain, too. Lots of it. But Royce pushed that pain as far back in his mind as he could and kept repeating to himself that they had to get out of this alive.

And then he'd learn the identity of every man hiding behind those ski masks.

Because this was going to stop.

The footsteps got closer, and despite the wind, Royce thought he might have heard whispers. The gunmen were no doubt trying to figure out the best way in. Royce hoped there wasn't one.

Sophie and he waited, but as time closed in around him, Royce began to think of some worst-case scenarios. Maybe the gunmen would try to use smoke or fire to draw them out. Just as Royce had done. He didn't have long to dwell on that thought, though.

There was a sharp cracking sound.

And a split second later, the door flew open.

Royce fired. But it was too late. The guy who'd kicked in the door dove to the right side of the barn, and the shot missed him.

Royce mumbled some profanity, and though he wanted to check on Sophie again, he didn't. He staked his attention on the now-open barn door and kept it there. He listened, trying to pick through the sound of the wind, his heartbeat and their breathing, so he could detect any movement.

He did.

Royce turned, took aim at the side of the barn where the gunman had landed. And he fired.

Royce's shot blistered through the air, the sound echoing through the barn, and he heard the groan of pain. And then the thud of a body hitting the ground. Royce waited, hoping the hit hadn't been faked, but then he heard something that confirmed it. One of the other gunmen cursed, and judging from his footsteps, he hurried toward his dead or injured partner.

"Stay down," he mouthed to Sophie in case the men tried to rush in. Or return fire.

Part of Royce hoped they'd just run away so that Sophie and he could escape, but that would mean this wouldn't end here. Until he had the person responsible, the attacks would just continue.

The phone in his pocket buzzed. Bad timing. Royce couldn't risk taking his attention off the front door to look at the screen and see who was calling, but this meant they now had cell service. Good to know if he managed to eliminate the two that were left, then he could call for help.

He kept listening, but Royce no longer heard the mumbles or profanity of the gunmen. No movement, either. And without the shots being fired, the silence closed in around them.

Royce didn't exactly get comfortable with the silence, but a jolt went through his body when he heard the crashing sound. He automatically glanced at the rear door, figuring their attackers were trying to get through there.

But there was no one.

His gaze slashed back to the front just as a gunman jumped out from cover. Royce fired at the same time there was more of that crashing noise. He pivoted, frantically looking around him, and he saw Sophie trying to scramble away from the gaping hole that was now in the side of the barn.

Someone had pulled off several of the rotting wooden planks.

And Royce got just a glimpse of the terror on Sophie's face as the person yanked her through the opening and out of the barn.

ONE SECOND SOPHIE WAS ON the barn floor, and the next she was being pulled outside.

Oh, God.

What was happening?

Yelling and kicking, she fought the person who was dragging her across the broken wood siding, but he was a lot stronger than she was. Plus, he'd had the element of surprise. By the time she'd realized what was happening to her, he had her out of the barn.

It was one of their attackers, but she couldn't see his face because of the ski mask.

Sophie landed hard on the cold ground, but she immediately tried to turn and aim the gun at her attacker. Again, he had the advantage of size and position, and he kicked the weapon from her hand. It went flying into the snow, and the pain screamed through her hand. At a minimum she would have bruises, but Sophie was afraid she might have broken bones. That wouldn't help her fight.

She didn't give up, though. Couldn't. Clearly her life was on the line here. Royce's, too, since he was already injured. She could hear him calling out to her, but she couldn't take the time to answer. She was in a fight for her life.

Sophie tried to scramble away from the gunman, toward the weapon he'd knocked from her hand. If she could get it, then at least she'd have some way to defend herself. But before she could even get close to it, the man latched on to her hair and dragged her to her feet.

"Sophie!" Royce shouted.

"Stay down," she warned him, and prayed he would listen.

Her attacker put her in front of him. Like a shield. And he shoved the gun against her head.

"Move and you die," he growled.

His voice was a hoarse whisper. One that she didn't recognize. Part of her was actually relieved that it wasn't her father or brother who'd launched this attack. Of course, that didn't mean one of them hadn't hired these men.

That hurt far more than the throbbing ache in her hand.

She shoved aside the physical pain and the thought. Right now it didn't matter who'd hired these men. It only mattered that Royce and she got out of this alive.

Sophie had some hope that it might be possible.

After all, the gunman hadn't immediately killed her when he pulled her out of the barn. He could have. Easily. In fact, he'd obviously known where she was, maybe because he'd heard her breathing or moving around inside, so he could have just fired through the rickety wall and ended her life. But he hadn't.

Why?

What did he want from Royce and her?

"McCall, make this easy on yourself and the woman," someone shouted. The other gunman, she realized. Judging from the sound of his voice, he was still somewhere near the front side of the barn.

"I've called for backup," Royce answered. "In a few minutes, cops will be crawling all over this place."

She figured that was a bluff, but it did seem

to unnerve the man who was holding her. He jammed the gun even harder against her head and started dragging her toward the front where she figured the other gunman was waiting.

"Let Sophie go," Royce said. "There's no reason for you to hold her."

"Yeah, there is," the man yelled. He paused, and she heard the whispered voice then.

Sophie glanced around, expecting to see yet another attacker, but she noticed the tiny communication device hooked into the ski mask near his ear.

"Will do," the man mumbled to that whispered voice.

So, there was someone else. *No.* The two gunmen were bad enough, but there was another culprit. One no doubt calling the shots. Maybe literally. Because while the gunman hadn't immediately put a bullet in her, she didn't think the same would be true for Royce.

"We have to leave with the woman now," the man holding her shouted to his partner. "Deputy McCall, that means you either surrender now or we start shooting. We got a lot of ammo, and those barn walls ain't gonna hold back many bullets. You want another shot in you, McCall?"

Royce didn't answer, but she could hear him moving around inside. *Mercy.* He wasn't surrendering, and she had no doubt that these men would do as they'd threatened.

"What do you want with Sophie?" Royce finally shouted.

She heard the whispered voice again.

"Business," her captor answered, no doubt repeating what he'd been told to say by the person on the other end of that communicator.

"Business that has to do with those papers you took from our SUV?" Royce added.

Yes, the papers. The ones that implicated her father, Travis and the other man in an illegal land deal. Was that what this was all about?

"I'm guessing Milton Wells is your boss," Royce continued. She could hear him moving inside, but she had no idea what he was doing. "I'm also guessing that Wells doesn't want anyone to find out who he really is."

The person on the communicator said something that Sophie wished she could hear because Royce seemed to be on the right track. Well, the right track for unnerving the man with the gun to her head.

"I have other copies of those papers," she tossed out there. It, too, was a bluff. There were no duplicates because she hadn't wanted other copies of the incriminating documents that could send her father to jail.

But her captor obviously didn't know that.

"We're taking her now," he shouted to his comrade after getting yet more whispered orders.

So that was it. The papers were the key to all of this, and if the duplicates actually existed, they would no doubt force her to hand them over.

And then they'd kill her.

"This is your last chance, McCall," the other gunman warned. "Surrender, and you'll live."

Sophie figured that was a lie, especially since the man holding her moved the gun and lifted it toward the barn.

Sweet heaven. They were going to start shooting.

She had to do something. She couldn't just stand there and let Royce be killed. Sophie adjusted her footing, preparing herself to drop down. She'd also try to elbow the man in the stomach. It wasn't much of a distraction, but maybe it would be enough for her to try to wrestle that gun away from him.

Sophie got ready, drew her elbow.

But before she could move an inch, she heard the movement behind them. Someone was running, and she saw the blur of motion from the corner of her eye.

Royce.

He came from the back of the barn and slammed his gun against her captor's head. He went down like a bag of rocks.

Royce immediately caught on to her. "Let's get out of here," he whispered.

They turned to run toward the house.

But they didn't get far.

Chapter Eighteen

Royce cursed when he saw the man step out from the back of the barn. The guy hadn't been there just seconds earlier when Royce had gone through the door to get to Sophie. But he was there now.

And he had a gun pointed right at Sophie and him.

Royce fired even though he was certain he didn't have a steady shot, and in the same motion, he dragged Sophie to the ground so she wouldn't be in the direct path if the guy returned fire.

He didn't.

It didn't take Royce long to realize why. The other gunman who'd been at the front of the barn now raced around the corner, behind Sophie and him. He was still armed, and he pointed his weapon at them.

Sophie and he were trapped.

Hell.

Royce had known it wasn't much of a plan for him to try to get her out of there, but he'd had to try. He couldn't just stand by while these goons kidnapped her.

And he was certain that's what they were planning to do.

Kidnap her and force her to tell them where those duplicate papers were that she'd hidden. Except he was pretty sure that the only copy of that land deal was now in the hands of the attacker who'd come from the back of the barn.

Royce covered Sophie's body with his. Trying to protect her. And he studied the man who was now making his way toward them. He didn't walk with the same air as the others. There was a confidence. No, make that arrogance.

This guy was the boss.

Too bad Royce couldn't see his face. Also too bad it could be any of their suspects. If he could pinpoint which one, he might have a better chance of negotiating their way out of this dangerous mess.

Especially if it was Eldon or Stanton.

Royce could maybe play the family card and remind them that Sophie was blood. It might also mean her life wasn't in as much danger as he'd thought it was since either Eldon or Stanton would probably indeed let her go once they made sure there were no other copies of those papers.

Other than an out-and-out escape, that was the best-case scenario here. For Sophie, anyway. The gunmen had already made it clear that they'd planned to kill him. Royce didn't think that they'd planned to kill him. Royce didn't think they would automatically change their minds about that, either. He was a loose end they couldn't afford to keep around.

The man in front of them aimed his gun. Not at Royce. But at Sophie, and he tipped his head to the gunman behind them.

"Put down your weapon," the lackey ordered Royce. "If not, I'll blow a hole in your lady friend's arm. It won't kill her, but it won't feel too good, either."

Royce glanced at both men, and there was nothing in their body language to indicate that was a bluff. They would indeed shoot Sophie. He had no choice but to toss his gun onto the ground, but he kept it close.

Still within reach.

Of course, either of those men could get off a shot before Royce could get his gun back in his hands, but maybe he could create some kind of distraction.

"Let Royce go," he heard Sophie say. "And I'll take you to the papers."

Royce cursed again and shot her a "stay quiet" glare.

Which she ignored.

"If you hurt him," she said to the man who stopped directly in front of them, "then I'll never give you those papers."

The man said nothing, but he did look at the other gunman who was behind Sophie and him.

"Want me to go ahead and take care of him?" the man asked his boss.

"No!" Sophie practically shouted. She pushed herself away from Royce, wriggling out from the meager cover that his body was providing for her, and she got to her feet. "I meant it. If Royce dies, you don't get what you want."

She looked back at Royce as he, too, got to his feet. There was worry etched on every part of her face and in her eyes, and that worry went up a huge notch when her attention landed on the blood on the jacket. The blood flow had slowed down significantly, thank God, but he was sure he looked like a man in need of serious medical attention.

"I'm so sorry," Sophie whispered to him, probably because she was still blaming herself for all of this.

But Royce was blaming the man in front of them.

"Let me guess," Royce said to that man. "You're Milton Wells, the guy who signed that illegal land deal. Of course Milton Wells is just an alias, isn't it?"

That wasn't exactly speculation since neither Kade Ryland nor Royce had been able to locate any info about the man.

"You're probably guessing—rightfully so— that eventually I'll figure out who Milton Wells really is," Royce added. "And that's why you want to kill me."

Sophie's eyes widened, and she tossed glances at all three of them. Hopefully, she realized now that it wouldn't do any good for her to go with them. If she did, it would just make it easier for them to kill her once they figured out that she couldn't give them what they wanted.

She turned back to the man in front of them, her gaze traveling from his head to his boots. No doubt trying to figure out if it was her brother behind that mask.

"It's either Stanton or Agent Lott," Royce said, going with his theory that this was some- one who'd posed as Milton Wells. "Because your father and Travis had already signed the docu- ment."

Of course, it could still be one of them, but Royce thought he saw a slight change in the boss's body language. Just a hint of movement that made Royce believe he'd hit the proverbial nail on the head.

"Lott," Royce said. "I know it's you." The man certainly didn't confirm it. Neither did his hired gun that still had a Glock pointed right at Sophie's arm. The seconds crawled by.

And the man finally cursed.

"This shouldn't have been this hard," he mumbled, adding more profanity. It was enough for Royce to recognize the speaker.

Agent Lott pulled off the mask, stuffing it into his jacket pocket. "If you think that knowing my identity will save you," Lott growled, "then think again. One way or another, I will get those papers from Sophie."

"Oh, mercy," she murmured.

She didn't sound relieved that it wasn't a family member trying to kill them, probably because she knew just how dangerous a rogue agent could be. Lott had the shooting skills and the backup to gun them both down. And Sophie and he didn't exactly have a lot going for them. No gun, and his shoulder was practically numb from the pain and blood loss.

But Royce had something Lott didn't.

The will to keep Sophie alive. The agent was doing this to cover his butt and his illegal activity, but Royce was fighting for Sophie's life.

"Sophie will go with you," Royce said to Lott.

It was a lie. Well, hopefully. Royce didn't want Lott to get Sophie out of his sight, but he needed one some kind of diversion. Better yet, he needed one or both of those guns aimed away from them.

Sophie shook her head and caught on to Royce's arm. "They'll kill you," she whispered.

They'd try. Royce would try to stop that, too.

He moved closer to Sophie, brushing his mouth over hers. "Play along," Royce whispered.

"Touching," Lott complained. "But I don't have time for a lovers' goodbye." He motioned with his gun for Sophie to follow him. "Come on."

She looked at Royce again, her eyes silently asking him what to do, and he glanced toward the side of the barn to that gaping hole. If possible, he wanted her through there. No, it wouldn't be much protection, but it might keep her out of the line of fire when he went for his gun on the ground.

Sophie gave a shaky nod, hopefully understanding what he wanted her to do. While he was hoping, Royce added that she would duck inside the barn for cover and not try to save him.

"Goodbye," she whispered. And then she turned as if she might indeed leave with Lott.

The agent reached out to take her arm. But he missed. Because Sophie screamed at the top of her voice and lunged toward the opening in the barn.

Royce dropped to the ground just as the shot blasted through the air.

SOPHIE DIDN'T HAVE TIME to make it through the hole in the barn. She'd tried to create a distraction by screaming, but it hadn't worked.

Lott had fired.

At Royce.

Without thinking, she turned and dove at the agent. Even though he was a lot larger than she was, she had speed and fury on her side. Sophie slammed into him, catching him off balance, and sending them both crashing to the ground.

Lott cursed, calling her a vile name, and he flipped her onto her back as if she weighed nothing. But Sophie didn't give up. She latched on to his right wrist with both of her hands and held on, digging her fingernails into his bare flesh.

She heard the movement. The scuffle. And she prayed that Royce hadn't been hit, that he was able to fight off the other gunman. But Royce was already hurt.

Maybe worse.

The thought of that broke her heart into a million little pieces. Royce had done so much to keep her safe, and here he was risking everything for her. That only made Sophie fight harder.

Lott fought harder, too. Probably because he knew if he didn't stop her and Royce that he'd spend the rest of his life in jail. Not a good outcome for a federal agent. He pinned her legs to the ground. Her body, as well. And he punched her in the jaw with his left hand.

The pain shot through her, and Sophie could have sworn she saw stars.

Somehow, despite the pain, she managed to hang on to Lott's wrist, and she clamped on the back of his hand with her teeth. Lott howled in pain and tried to bash her away from him.

Even over the roaring in her ears, Sophie heard Royce. He was cursing, too. And then she heard something she didn't want to hear.

A cracking sound.

And someone yelled in pain.

Because the adrenaline and the pain were pumping through her, it took her several moments to figure out that it wasn't Royce who had yelled but the other gunman.

She looked past Lott, not easy to do with him trying to wrestle his shooting hand away from her, and she saw Royce coming directly toward them. He had his gun in his hand, and in addition to his shoulder, his head was bleeding.

"Stay back!" Lott yelled.

Until he said that, Sophie hadn't known that Lott had seen Royce, too. But he had. Lott bashed her in the face again, and when her head flopped back, he snapped his left arm around her and dragged them to a standing position. Even though she kept hold of his wrist, that didn't stop

Lott from twisting the gun until it was pointed at Royce.

"If you keep struggling, Sophie," Lott said. "Royce dies here and now."

Lott left no room for doubt in his voice, so Sophie's grip melted off his wrist.

Now that she was facing Royce, she had no trouble seeing all the nicks and cuts on his face—no doubt from the fight with the gunman. She hadn't heard a shot, so Royce had probably knocked the guy unconscious. That was good except for the fact that Lott still controlled the situation. As long as he had Royce in the crosshairs of his gun, she couldn't do anything to risk him shooting.

Royce was just a few feet in front of them.

There was no way Lott could miss.

"It doesn't have to be this way," Royce said. He kept his gun aimed at Lott, but she doubted he had a clean shot because she was literally in his line of fire.

"It does," Lott argued. He tightened his grip on Sophie and started to back away. He was trying to escape with her.

No!

That couldn't happen. She might be able to stall him for a little while, but eventually he'd kill her. Of course, her more immediate concern was for Royce.

He followed Lott and her.

"You'll get some jail time," Royce tried again. "And with a good lawyer, maybe not even much of that."

She felt Lott shake his head. "Travis is dead. I killed him, but I haven't had time to set up the evidence to frame you."

"Travis is dead?" Sophie asked.

"Yeah. He was blackmailing me about that land deal. Not a good idea."

That robbed her of her breath. Not because Sophie cared for Travis. No, he was scum. But it meant Lott was a killer now. First-degree murder, and he would no doubt do anything to make sure he wasn't arrested for something that would get him the death penalty. It let her know just how desperate, and dangerous, this man was.

"Hard to set me up for a murder when I'm dead," Royce reminded him.

"Hard, yes, but it's doable," Lott argued. "When those two men regain consciousness, they'll clean up the mess and plant your body where it needs to be. It'll look as if you got into a gunfight with Travis."

Royce shook his head. "If Travis is already dead, that'll be a tough sell. A good CSI will be able to determine that the times of death don't match."

"Yeah, if it weren't for this cold weather."

God, that was probably true. Besides, as a federal agent, Lott knew how to stage the evidence. That's why Sophie had to do something.

But what?

She'd already lost one scuffle with Lott, and while Royce was still armed, he was hurt and didn't look too steady on his feet. And then Sophie saw something that made their situation go from bad to worse.

One of the gunmen on the ground groaned and stirred. It wouldn't be long before he got up, ready to help his boss commit another murder or two.

"Plus, you have other loose ends," Royce said. He, too, was keeping an eye on those men. "That confidential informant you told us about. What if he gets scared and tells all?"

"He won't know to tell," Lott answered. "Because he didn't know he was an informant. It was Stanton, and I had him followed. That's how I knew he'd drugged Sophie and you."

"And I guess it didn't occur to you to stop him?" Sophie asked.

Lott lifted his shoulder. "Sometimes, those things play out in a man's favor. I figured if Stanton accidentally killed one of you with a drug overdose, I could blackmail him into doing whatever I wanted—including getting me those papers."

He was beyond sick. Their lives were nothing to him. And with his two goons stirring and ready to get up, Lott would no doubt unleash them first on Royce.

Then, her.

Sophie didn't think. Without warning, she dropped down, jerking Lott down with her. They didn't hit the ground like before, but he wobbled.

Royce dove at them.

He pushed Sophie out of the way and rammed right into Lott. They fell onto the ground, and the fight started instantly. Both of them were jockeying for position and trying to disarm the other.

Sophie hated the thought of Royce being injured further, but she had to do something to stop that gunman who was already trying to sit up. She raced to her gun, scooped it up and pointed it right at him.

"Move and I'll shoot," she warned, and it wasn't a bluff. She would indeed shoot the man rather than let him try to help his boss.

Sophie gathered both of the gunmen's weapons and tossed them inside the hole in the barn wall. That freed up her hands so that she could keep her own gun aimed and maybe help Royce.

Lott and he were delivering punches. Hard ones. And Sophie nearly screamed when she saw blood fly through the air and land on the snow. Royce already had too many injuries, and

God knows what this was doing to his gunshot wound.

It could be killing him.

She stood there, volleying glances between the gunmen and the fight. Trying to decide what to do. Her head racing. Her heart was pounding. Her head racing with the worst thoughts possible.

She couldn't lose Royce.

Sophie was ready to dive into the fray, but the sound stopped her cold.

A thick blast.

It echoed through the air. Through her. And it made her blood turn to ice.

That's because someone, either Lott or Royce, had fired the shot.

Her breath vanished, and it took every ounce of her willpower just to stay on her feet. She prayed. Waited. And she saw Royce roll off Lott and to the side. He landed hard on his back on the ground.

She kept her gun pointed at the gunmen, but she ran to him, terrified of what she might see. There was more blood. Too much. And for several horrifying moments, she thought he'd been shot again.

"I'm okay," Royce said, his breath gusting.

Sophie shook her head, not believing him. He couldn't be okay, not with all that blood on his jacket.

Royce got to his feet, not easily, but she latched on to his arm and helped him get up. That's when she realized Lott hadn't moved. She looked down at the agent and spotted the source of the blood.

On Lott's chest.

He wasn't moving, and his eyes were fixed in a blank, dead stare.

"It's all right," Royce whispered to her. He took the gun from her, aimed it at the gunmen, and with his left arm he pulled her to him. "It's all right," he repeated.

And Sophie was on the verge of believing him.

Until she felt Royce collapse against her.

Chapter Nineteen

Royce tried not to make any sounds of pain or discomfort while the nurse stitched him up. That's because he knew Sophie was in the exam room next to him, and he didn't want her to hear anything else today that would add to her already raw nerves.

His nerves were certainly raw, too. Partly because of the attack that could have easily left Sophie and him dead. Also because he was berating himself for falling for the stupid ruse that Lott had created. The dirty agent had said he was going to arrest Sophie's father because he'd known it would send them racing back to town on the only road they could have used to get to Mustang Ridge.

It had turned out to be a bad mistake.

And it had nearly cost him Sophie.

That in itself was bad enough, but now Royce's nerves were raw for a different reason. When Dr. Amos Jenkins had taken Sophie into the adjoining room to examine her, Royce had been able to hear them talking. He hadn't heard exactly what they were saying, but just the sound of Sophie's murmurings had given Royce some reassurance that even though she was shaken up, she was okay.

But he could no longer hear her.

Royce tried to assure himself that's because the exam had gone well and there was nothing else for Dr. Jenkins to say to her. However, his thoughts were moving in a different direction, too. That something was wrong. That she'd had an injury that he hadn't noticed on the way to the hospital. There'd been plenty of chances for that to happen.

"Can you hurry?" he asked the nurse, Alice Wilkins. It wasn't his first request but his third, and he made it clear he would keep asking until she'd finished.

Maybe that's why she made a sound of disapproval. "Hold your horses. I'm working as fast as I can." She added another stitch. "You were lucky."

Yeah, the doctor and X-ray tech had already said the same thing. The shot to his shoulder had been a through and through. But Royce didn't feel lucky, and he wouldn't until he'd made sure that Sophie was okay.

It seemed to take hours, but the nurse finally

finished with his shoulder and started in on the cuts on his head. Those would have to wait. He'd used up all the patience he had, and Royce eased the nurse aside, got off the table and headed for the door.

"I'll be back," he told her, but that might not be the truth. He'd be back only after he saw Sophie.

Royce bolted out the door and nearly ran smack-dab into his brother. "Whoa," Jake said, backing up. "In a hurry?"

"Where's Sophie?" But Royce didn't wait for an answer. He went to the examining room and threw open the door.

Empty.

"She went to the bathroom," Jake supplied. "She's all right."

Yeah, and Royce might believe that once he saw her for himself.

Jake caught on to him when Royce started down the hall. "Dr. Amos told Sophie and me that you were okay, that your injuries weren't too bad and you were just getting stitched up."

"They aren't bad," Royce agreed. "What did he say about Sophie's injuries?"

"They're minor. Just a few cuts and bruises. She was a little queasy, though, and that's why she wanted to go to the bathroom."

Hell. Queasy didn't sound good for several reasons. Maybe the pregnancy. Maybe an injury the doctor hadn't detected. Even if it was simply because she was upset—and she had a right to feel that—Royce didn't want her going through that alone.

"Hey." Jake stopped him again when he started to leave. "What's going on? Did something happen that you didn't tell me about?"

Nothing that had to do with the investigation. Royce had filled in his brother when Jake had arrived at the vacant farm and driven them back to Mustang Ridge. In turn, Jake had taken over tying up a few loose ends, like charging the surviving gunmen and starting the paperwork.

"I'm not blind," Jake said, keeping a grip on Royce's arm. "I saw the way you were holding Sophie in the truck."

He'd done some holding all right. In fact, Royce hadn't wanted to let go of her. It might take a lifetime or two for him to forget the bullets flying past her and the way the SOB Lott had punched her in the face.

"You care for her," Jake added.

"I do," Royce admitted. And it was a relief to say it aloud.

However, his relief was cut short when he heard the hurried footsteps and he saw Stanton making a beeline toward them.

"I heard," Stanton said. "Is Sophie hurt?" Royce was about to say he didn't know and head out to find her, but he saw the movement at the end of the hall and spotted her coming out of the bathroom.

His breath of relief was a lot louder than he'd anticipated, and it caused both Jake and Stanton to give him a funny look. Royce ignored them and went to her. Sophie moved quickly toward him, too, and they pulled each other into their arms.

She held him gently, mindful of his wounded shoulder, but Royce brought her even closer to him.

"The doctor said you'd be okay." Her voice was all breath, and she was trembling. She held him so gently that he figured she was terrified of hurting him.

But nothing hurt now.

Well, except for seeing those bruises on her face and chin. Royce wished he could give Lott another beating for those. It took a special kind of scum to hit a woman.

He pushed her hair from her face so he could examine every nick, every scrape, and yeah, those god-awful bruises.

"Nothing serious," she assured him but frowned when her attention landed on his bandaged shoulder. "You shouldn't be on your feet."

Royce ignored that. "Jake said you were queasy."

She nodded, glanced around, nodded again and looked as if she might say something. And then Sophie's attention landed on her brother who was making his way toward them.

"Stanton." She eased away from Royce and hugged him.

"I heard what Lott did to you," Stanton cursed. "I'm glad the bastard's dead." He lifted her chin, examining the bruises, and had a reaction similar to Royce's.

Even though Royce still wasn't happy about Stanton drugging them, it seemed as if he really did care for Sophie. And that meant Royce would figure out a way to forgive him. Sophie could no doubt do the same since he was family and she loved him.

"Royce is the one who's hurt," she said, stepping away from her brother. "He saved my life. Several times," she added, her voice breaking now.

Royce pulled her back in his arms. "She saved mine a couple of times, too."

"I'm thankful for that," Stanton said, and he glanced back at Jake. "Your brother doesn't know yet, but our father turned himself in for the illegal land deal." He paused, met Sophie's gaze. "He'll no doubt have to do some jail time."

Royce braced himself for her reaction. She didn't burst into tears, maybe because of the spent adrenaline and bone-weary fatigue but she gave a heavy sigh and ran her hand down her brother's arm.

"I can hire a lawyer for him." Sophie shook her head. "But I can't save the ranch."

Stanton's sigh was heavy, too. "I didn't expect you to." He gently kissed her cheek. "And maybe that's not such a bad thing. Don't know about you, but I'm looking forward to a clean start."

Yeah. So was Royce. But he wasn't sure Sophie and he had a shot at that. Too much old baggage. Maybe too much new baggage, as well.

"I'll go to the sheriff's office and check on Dad," Stanton said. "I'll let him know you're okay."

"Thanks. I'll be there later myself."

"Are you sure you're up for that?" Royce asked.

She nodded but waited until her brother had walked away before she added anything. "I love my father. Always will. But I can't undo what he's done, and he needs to pay for that."

Maybe her change of heart had come because she'd seen firsthand just what illegal activity could do. After all, Lott wouldn't have had a reason to try to kill them if it hadn't been for her father's land deal.

"I'll see my father," she explained. "But then I think he and I need some space."

Royce figured that wouldn't be a pleasant meeting, and he intended to be there. Well, after he got something else out of the way.

"What about the queasiness?" Royce asked.

Sophie glanced around as if to make sure no one was close by. No one was. Even Jake was still waiting up the hall, probably to give them some time alone. She took the small pen from her pocket. At least Royce thought it was a pen, but then he had a closer look.

"A pregnancy test?" he asked.

"I got it from one of the nurses I know." She dodged his gaze. "It only takes two minutes, she said."

Two minutes. Not long at all.

Royce reminded himself that they needed to know and they would have already had it done if it hadn't been for the attacks. But suddenly a big knot formed in his stomach.

"I can take you somewhere so you can do the test," he offered.

She tipped her head to the ladies' room just a few doors down. "Or I can do it here."

Yeah. *Here.* Which would mean that two minutes was actually two minutes and wouldn't include a trip that would delay the results.

"Let me tell Jake that it's okay for him to leave," Royce said.

She nodded. And Royce saw it then. Her

nerves just beneath the surface. He wasn't the only one with a stomach in knots.

He went back to Jake, trying not to look as if his entire world was suddenly up in the air. "Why don't you go on back to the office, and I'll join you there?"

Jake glanced at Sophie and then at him. "No, you won't. Whatever's going on between you two, you need to settle it."

He thought of the pregnancy test. Well, that would settle it.

Or would it?

Even if Sophie *was* pregnant, that didn't mean she'd want him in her life. Hell, she might not want him, *period*. He'd told her she wasn't his type. Had harped on the fact of his own parents' bad marriage. Yeah, she was attracted to him.

He was attracted to her.

But that didn't mean anything was *settled*.

"Take some time off," Jake insisted. "And before you kiss her again, you might want to wash the blood off your face. Most women don't find a bloody cheek very romantic."

It was exactly the kind of lighthearted brotherly ribbing he needed. Jake hadn't had to say he would support him no matter what—Royce knew that he would.

Drawing in a long breath, Royce headed back down the hall, and he caught Sophie by the arm as they walked to the ladies' room. "I'm going in with you," he insisted.

She stopped so fast he nearly tripped over her. "It's the *ladies'* room," she emphasized. "And you know what I have to do on this thing, right?"

"That's what I figured," He saw her point then. Most women wouldn't have wanted a man around for that. "I'll wait right outside the door."

Sophie nodded, seemed relieved. "The nurse said if we get a plus sign, I'm pregnant. A negative sign means I'm not."

Simple enough. The makers of the test probably made it that way because they figured some people might be crazy in this situation.

Sophie turned to go inside the bathroom. Royce stopped her and kissed her. Not one of those gentle pecks he'd given her earlier. Not a kiss of relief, either. The kiss he would give his lover.

Because Sophie was.

She had a slight smile when she eased back and ran her tongue over her bottom lip. The concern quickly returned, but before he could kiss it away again, she ducked inside.

Royce considered a quick trip to the men's room to wash his face as Jake had suggested, but the next few seconds suddenly seemed a lot more than two minutes.

He paced. Checked his watch. And then put his ear to the door to listen.

"I need you to time this," he heard her say.

Royce cursed. Heck, the two minutes hadn't even started yet. He fastened his attention to his watch. Or rather tried. And he gave up and opened the door.

Sophie was there standing by the sink where she'd placed the little white stick.

"Anyone else in here?" he asked.

She shook her head. And Royce stepped inside with her. He glanced at the test. The screen was still blank. A clean slate, so to speak.

And that's when it hit him.

He didn't want a clean slate on either the test or his life. He wanted Sophie. Royce caught on to her and turned her to face him so he could tell her that.

"It'll be okay," she whispered.

"Yeah." Maybe it would be. Their gazes connected, and he pulled her into his arm for another kiss. "Sophie, I'm in love with you."

She blinked and made a sound a drunk person might make. "W-what?"

Royce tried not to panic, but he'd hoped she would jump into his arms and tell him that she loved him, too. Well, she wasn't jumping. She was staring at him with her mouth open.

"I know, it's sudden," he tried.

But she pressed her fingers over his lips. "No. It's not. We've lived a few lifetimes in the last few days. It's not sudden at all." She swallowed hard. "And I'm in love with you, too."

At first, it felt as if someone had slugged him. The air sort of swooshed out of him. Hardly a manly reaction. But the breath returned. So did the relief. And he hauled her into his arms. Gently, of course. Because of their injuries. And the kiss he gave her was gentle, too.

"Marry me," he said with his mouth against hers.

She pulled back again. "If you're doing this because of the test—"

"I'm not. In fact, I don't want you to look at that test until you've answered me. Will you marry me, Sophie?"

Tears sprang to her eyes.

The door sprang open, too.

"Sorry," Royce said to the woman who was about to come in. "Official police business."

He shut the door, held it closed with his foot and turned back to Sophie. "Well?"

"You said I wasn't right for you." She didn't wait for him to correct that falsehood. "But I am. And you're the right man for me."

Yeah. That was the response he wanted, and the kiss she gave him wasn't too shabby, either.

"Well?" he pressed. "I need an answer to my proposal."

"Yes," she said before he even finished. And she repeated her yes a couple of times.

Royce couldn't help himself. He whooped for joy and probably scared some folks out in the hall. He didn't care. Right now, the only thing that mattered was that Sophie loved him and she'd said multiple yeses.

The next kiss was considerably longer and hotter than it should have been, considering they weren't close enough to a bed to finish it off the right away. They pulled back, breathless and revved up.

"We should celebrate," he suggested, "in bed."

"Are you up to that?" She glanced at his shoulder, at his sly smile, and gave him a smile of her own.

"Always," Royce assured her.

First, though, they had to look at the test stick on the sink. It no longer seemed as life altering as it had been just ten minutes ago. In fact, either way it went, Royce would be happy because if Sophie wasn't pregnant, he'd do something about getting her that way real quick.

Without looking at the little screen, she scooped up the test and held it for him to see. Sophie kept her gaze nailed to his.

And this time Royce didn't just smile. He laughed.

The little pink plus sign was crystal clear. Royce pulled her back to him. "I need to get you to the altar right away," he said. He turned the test so she could see it.

Sophie blinked, but the smile came just as quickly. The laugh, too. "Are you ready for this?" she asked, blinking back happy tears.

"Oh, yeah," he drawled. Royce figured Sophie and he were in for one heck of a good life.

* * * * *

Look for more books from USA TODAY
bestselling author Delores Fossen when her
brand-new miniseries,
THE MARSHALS OF MAVERICK COUNTY,
launches in May 2013.
You'll find them wherever
Harlequin Intrigue books are sold!

LARGER-PRINT BOOKS!
GET 2 FREE LARGER-PRINT NOVELS PLUS
2 FREE GIFTS!

⊞ HARLEQUIN®

INTRIGUE®

BREATHTAKING ROMANTIC SUSPENSE

YES! Please send me 2 FREE LARGER-PRINT Harlequin Intrigue® novels and my 2 FREE gifts (gifts are worth about $10). After receiving them, if I don't wish to receive any more books, I can return the shipping statement marked "cancel." If I don't cancel, I will receive 6 brand-new novels every month and be billed just $5.24 per book in the U.S. or $5.99 per book in Canada. That's a saving of at least 13% off the cover price! It's quite a bargain! Shipping and handling is just 50¢ per book in the U.S. and 75¢ per book in Canada.* I understand that accepting the 2 free books and gifts places me under no obligation to buy anything. I can always return a shipment and cancel at any time. Even if I never buy another book, the two free books and gifts are mine to keep forever.

199/399 HDN FV07

Name _____ (PLEASE PRINT) _____

Address _____ Apt. #

City _____ State/Prov. _____ Zip/Postal Code

Signature (if under 18, a parent or guardian must sign)

Mail to the **Harlequin® Reader Service:**
IN U.S.A.: P.O. Box 1867, Buffalo, NY 14240-1867
IN CANADA: P.O. Box 609, Fort Erie, Ontario L2A 5X3

Are you a subscriber to Harlequin Intrigue books and want to receive the larger-print edition?
Call 1-800-873-8635 today or visit www.ReaderService.com.

* Terms and prices subject to change without notice. Prices do not include applicable taxes. Sales tax applicable in N.Y. Canadian residents will be charged applicable taxes. Offer not valid in Quebec. This offer is limited to one order per household. Not valid for current subscribers to Harlequin Intrigue Larger-Print books. All orders subject to credit approval. Credit or debit balances in a customer's account(s) may be offset by any other outstanding balance owed by or to the customer. Please allow 4 to 6 weeks for delivery. Offer available while quantities last.

Your Privacy—The Harlequin® Reader Service is committed to protecting your privacy. Our Privacy Policy is available online at www.ReaderService.com or upon request from the Harlequin Reader Service.

We make a portion of our mailing list available to reputable third parties that offer products we believe may interest you. If you prefer that we not exchange your name with third parties, or if you wish to clarify or modify your communication preferences, please visit us at www.ReaderService.com/consumerschoice or write to us at Harlequin Reader Service Preference Service, P.O. Box 9062, Buffalo, NY 14269. Include your complete name and address.

HILP13

ReaderService.com

Manage your account online!

- Review your order history
- Manage your payments
- Update your address

*We've designed
the Harlequin® Reader Service
website just for you.*

Enjoy all the features!

- Reader excerpts from any series
- Respond to mailings and special monthly offers
- Discover new series available to you
- Browse the Bonus Bucks catalog
- Share your feedback

Visit us at:
ReaderService.com

REQUEST YOUR FREE BOOKS!

2 FREE NOVELS
PLUS 2 FREE GIFTS!

MYSTERY

W(O)RLDWIDE LIBRARY®

™

Your Partner in Crime

YES! Please send me 2 FREE gifts (gifts are worth about $10,) and my 2 FREE novels from the Worldwide Library® series and to receive any more books, I can return the shipping statement marked "cancel." If I don't cancel, I will receive 4 brand-new novels every month and be billed just $5.24 per book in the U.S. or $6.24 per book in Canada. That's a savings of at least 34% off the cover price. It's quite a bargain! Shipping and handling is just 50¢ per book in the U.S. and 75¢ per book in Canada. * I understand that accepting the 2 free books and gifts places me under no obligation to buy anything. I can always return a shipment and cancel at any time. Even if I never buy another book, the two free books and gifts are mine to keep forever.

414/424 WDN FVUV

Name	(PLEASE PRINT)
Address	Apt. #
City	State/Prov.	Zip/Postal Code

Signature (if under 18, a parent or guardian must sign)

Mail to the Harlequin® Reader Service:
IN U.S.A.: P.O. Box 1867, Buffalo, NY 14240-1867
IN CANADA: P.O. Box 609, Fort Erie, Ontario L2A 5X3

Want to try two free books from another line?
Call 1-800-873-8635 or visit www.ReaderService.com.

* Terms and prices subject to change without notice. Prices do not include applicable taxes. Sales tax applicable in N.Y. Canadian residents will be charged applicable taxes. Offer not valid in Quebec. This offer is limited to one order per household. Not valid for current subscribers to the Worldwide Library series. All orders subject to credit approval. Credit or debit balances in a customer's account(s) may be offset by any other outstanding balance owed by or to the customer. Please allow 4 to 6 weeks for delivery. Offer available while quantities last.

Your Privacy—The Harlequin® Reader Service is committed to protecting your privacy. Our Privacy Policy is available online at www.ReaderService.com or upon request from the Harlequin Reader Service.

We make a portion of our mailing list available to reputable third parties that offer products we believe may interest you. If you prefer that we not exchange your name with third parties, or if you wish to clarify or modify your communication preferences, please visit us at www.ReaderService.com/consumerschoice or write to us at Harlequin Reader Service Preference Service, P.O. Box 9062, Buffalo, NY 14269. Include your complete name and address.

WWL13